Three Musketeers

Marcelo Birmajer

Three Musketeers

TRANSLATED BY

Sharon Wood

The Toby Press

Three Musketeers

The Toby Press LLC
First English Edition, 2008

The Toby Press LLC

POB 8531, New Milford, CT 06776-8531, USA
& POB 2455, London WIA 5WY, England
www.tobypress.com

First published in Spanish as *Tres Mosqueteros*
Copyright © Marcelo Birmajer, 2001

The right of Marcelo Birmajer to be identified as the author
of this work has been asserted by him in accordance
with the Copyright, Designs & Patents Act 1988

Translation © Sharon Wood, 2008

ISBN 978 1 59264 193 2, *hardcover*

A CIP catalogue record for this title is
available from the British Library

Typeset by Koren Publishing Services

Printed and bound in the United States

For my beloved wife Débora
For my mother and my grandmother
In memory of my dear friend Fabiàn Polosecki

Chapter one

It's quite simple, Mossen,' said señor Pesce. 'You've got to do something.'

'But señor Pesce,' I replied, 'you know my thing is feature writing.'

Neither señor Pesce nor I had a very clear idea of what my 'thing' was, if truth be told. For a couple of years now I'd managed to slide unobtrusively around the newspaper without anyone managing to pin me down to one particular job or another.

My tactic for slipping through señor Pesce's fingers was to counter all of his demands with what I would term 'habitual satire.' By this I mean a kind of false literary habit, a cult whose inventor and greatest exponent is the Argentinian writer Adolfo Bioy Casares.

Between the sheet of glass and the blue wood of my bedside table I had stuck an A4 size piece of paper with twenty-five of Bioy's phrases, so I could bring them out in any sudden emergency Rodolfo Pesce might confront me with. The only one I had managed to memorise word for word was, however, unusable. I had taken it from the short story called 'The Shortcut', and it was a perfect line. Two people living in a small town in the province of Buenos Aires are captured by a foreign army—in the pay of some future tyrant—and just as they are about to be shot, Guzmá says to Batiliana:

'I can see your wife.'

It was an epigram of devastating limpidity, but—when on earth could I use it with Pesce? I wasn't even sure Pesce had a wife for me to see. Indeed, I knew nothing about his sexual habits. There was nothing in his behaviour to give me a clue. Pesce was cautious, pale, his mouth framed by two thick lips, the upper one of which protruded slightly. He gave the impression of being a man who wouldn't be the slightest bit bothered if you said to him:

'I can see your wife.'

It wasn't even beyond the realm of possibility that he would quite like me to see his wife.

I never managed to commit the rest of Bioy's verbal quips, handwritten and placed by my bed, to memory. Nonetheless that very reply, which had popped unexpectedly into my head, was just what I needed.

'My thing, señor Pesce, is feature writing.'

Pesce peered at me closely as if to catch me out, to prove to himself and to me that I was making fun of him. However, I wasn't about to be caught.

He didn't like me calling him 'señor.' But what could he say about that?

I was showing him respect.

In any case, my private mocking of Pesce still didn't protect me from his authority. Pesce could send me off to cover whatever story he wanted, from reporting on the recently elected treasurer of the Argentine authors' society, to the watercolour given as a retirement gift to the chief of the local volunteer firefighters.

This time, Pesce wanted me to interview Elías Traúm.

Chapter two

The piece on Elías Traúm brought together two themes, one vast, the other beyond comprehension. The fate of the 'foquistas', the revolutionaries inspired by Che Guevara, in the 1960s—basically the left-wing Montonero Peronist guerilla group, which two friends of Eliás, now dead, had belonged to—and Judaism. Or Jews. Or the endless array of Jewish Judaisms.

The Montoneros had always seemed like a bunch of clowns to me. Some of them were bloodthirsty, others just crazily naïve. I found them very distasteful.

Various colleagues of mine had belonged to the Montoneros when they were younger, and I was on pretty good terms with some of them. But in each case we knew that discussion about their political past was a no-go area. I refused to concede them the gift of ignorance, or indeed of innocence or youth. I knew some of them had lost friends, and even that one or two of them had suffered in body and soul the horrors of the military dungeons. But my gaze over their past was pitiless, and I saw no reason for it to be any other way.

The other area I had to ask Traúm about—Judaism—left me a bit flat. Personally, I'd had thirty-two years of Judaism. After a normal

3

Jewish childhood, I had dedicated my adolescence to turning myself into a layman. Adulthood found me attempting to recover my Jewish roots. And I was at the exact point where any question about myself was unwelcome. Obviously I was a Jew, and obviously I was a layman. How could I make it any plainer? What could I talk to señor Traúm about without being bored out of my mind?

Late in life I had discovered that nothing takes us so far away from a possible truth as the business of 'looking for ourselves.'

The strange thing about this supposed introspective search is that when we set out on it we believe our soul to be a calm continent, an unchanging space, peacefully waiting for us to totter across it. The only thing we can be sure of is that nobody knows who he is. We are barely what we do, and our actions vary hugely when there is the faintest hint that we might ascribe to them any sort of certainty about who we all are.

Nobody knows who he is, and as such the best thing is to proceed cautiously through life and not get our hopes up too much. Maybe paradise is simply the place where we will be handed a leaflet telling us clearly who we are, what we wanted and why we couldn't have it.

At thirty-two years of age, my Judaism had congealed into an unimpeachable love for the modern state of Israel. This was all that was left after thirty years of wandering around in the desert of doubt.

It suited me this way.

This belief allowed me to distance myself regularly from the progressives of every hue. You couldn't have dinner or even just a coffee with one of these progressive types without them finding some excuse or another to start slagging off Israel. On these occasions I unleashed all my power of argument. I would give my progressive such a verbal roasting that he would be severed not only from his subject but also from the desire ever to see me again. I was particularly firm with the Jewish progressives who found their spiritual and political serenity by projecting all their self-hatred onto a country that was younger than the province of Tucumán.

I asked nothing more of myself. And neither did I want to ask anything of Traúm. All I asked of Providence was to be left in peace.

By dint of real effort I had managed to make for myself an official subterfuge: wandering around the newspaper offices offering the various section chiefs an always pliable and biddable pen. I didn't want to do any pieces that might mean me 'getting involved.'

I had no time for people in any line of work who felt themselves somehow compromised by what they did. Any real possibility of compromise should begin by being completely alien to us.

And so my dear señor Traúm, my dear señor Pesce, I, the still youthful yet weary Jew, Mossen, am not the right man to write a thousand lines for the Sunday supplement on a history of blood and belief.

'It's perfectly straightforward, Mossen,' said señor Pesce. 'You're doing it.'

Chapter three

Traúm lived in Israel and was arriving at the airport at twelve-thirty, midday, on an El Al flight. I went to meet him.

He wasn't coming for this piece particularly. Somebody in the office knew him, was in touch with him and knew what day and time he was getting there.

'So why don't you give the piece to the journalist who knew about señor Traúm coming, señor Pesce?'

Pesce refused to tell me the name of the journalist who had suggested doing the article.

'Because he's not a Jew, Mossen. He wouldn't understand a thing.'

'I'm surprised at you, señor Pesce. Do you think only a Jew can interview another Jew?'

'You know what it's all about, Mossen. Weren't you the one who did the piece on Ioram Beemet?'

Of course, damn it, I'd written the article on the Dutch-Jewish writer Ioram Beemet. I'd also written the piece on the opening night of an Israeli play at the national theatre. With this third piece on

Traúm, the Jew Mossen would completely bring down the curtains on his literary and journalistic ghetto.

'Will you cover the scandal of the kosher meat, Mossen?'

'Mossen, what do you know about the circumcision of that Jewish boy?'

'Mossen, have you got a spare moment to write a column in response to the journalist who said there was no such thing as a Jewish cuisine?'

Yes indeed, Mossen was rushing headlong to turn himself into a gentile newspaper's decorative Star of David. This was the unavoidable alternative for the children of Israel in exile, wallowing in the oasis of a tolerant newspaper.

'Mossen, you don't normally make a fuss about the pieces you do,' said Pesce. 'We change what you write, we make you say things that would never have occurred to you. We even knock out every line where any idea even slightly out of sync with the ideological tenor of the paper might show through. And you never turn a hair. What's the matter, Mossen? What are you afraid of?'

Now it was Pesce who was on the attack. He was the one who was mocking me on the sly. His boldness cheered me. His audacity made me smile. Mocking a fool is the job of cowards. But, and señor Pesce must surely acknowledge this point, so is mocking a subordinate. My elliptical jibe carried greater weight than his.

Whatever. I enjoyed the cab ride out to Ezeiza airport. The freeway seemed to me one of the great technological advances in Argentina. And although many things had lost their flavour for me over the past few years, airports were not one of them. Airports summoned up in me that je ne sais quoi which makes us happy, recalling joyful moments from our childhood or a date with a woman we thought would never happen. These occasional and always fragile proofs that it is possible to live. I loved the frenetic rhythm of airports, the fact that they never stopped day or night, the euphoria of people as they came or left, the tears of those left behind, the embraces of those who returned, the smell of the rubberised floor, the automatic doors, the intact beauty of the air hostesses who were on their way out and the weary beauty of the crew when they returned. Why hadn't I become an air steward? Maybe because that had always been my brother's dream, while he ended up as an accountant working for the state. My favourite time of all in an airport was midday. I liked the ham and cheese rolls on the bar counter where you stand and drink coffee.

Once my brother, the public accountant, said:

'I'd like to get back all the money I ever spent in my life, everything I spent on clothes, food, cinema. A miracle, and I'd get the lot back. Except what I spent on travelling. I don't want that back—that was money well spent.'

Traúm had spent his money on a trip to Argentina and nobody was going to give it back to him. Indeed, a much more likely scenario was that he would be relieved of a large part of his cash by some arcane customs manoeuvre or by the cab driver.

I was there to stop this happening. Nobody else had gone to meet señor Traúm. Only the Jew Mossen with a white piece of cardboard with some writing which looked like it had been written by a kid in primary school, spelling out the name of Eliás Traúm.

Why had I been so sparing in making my placard of greeting? Why hadn't I put 'Señor Traúm, we love you'? Or perhaps less showy but no less heartfelt: 'Welcome, Eliás Traúm.'

I'd done my best.

A young lady's voice over the loudspeaker announced the arrival of the plane.

A few moments later the passengers started to file out.

For a second I forgot what I was there for, as I imagined what the girl who had just announced the landing of the El Al flight would be like in bed.

I didn't even attempt to imagine her body or her face. Just that—what would she be like in bed?

Would she let herself be sodomised? Would she like to be sodomised against her will? Not necessarily in bed: I imagined her sitting on a chair, announcing arrivals and departures over the microphone, while I watched her with my trousers down, standing by her side, giving her the option to invite me to sit down under her.

When I looked up again, for I had been outlining the scene while staring at a cigarette paper stuck to the rubber floor, I saw the name of señor Traúm on another piece of board.

The passengers were coming out—men and women looking slightly bewildered, loaded down with their hand luggage and trolleys full of bags and cases, looking for all the world like immigrants of bygone times. Suddenly a whole swarm of placards were thrust into the air as if we were welcoming political leaders.

Cab drivers were shouting and pushing in search of their prey. They took no notice of waiting family or children. They yelled: 'Shall I take that, sir? Cab, young lady? Cab, sir?' They were a savage urban tribe and a whiff of mafia drifted about them.

The face with its coplike moustache and the plastic jacket revealed that the man carrying the placard with the same name on it as mine was a cab driver. The letters on his card were those of an adult, and although they were not printed they had something of the typewriter about them. I went over to him while not taking my eyes off the emerging passengers, keeping my pathetic card well in view.

'I've come to meet Eliás Traúm, too,' I said to him.

The cab driver looked at me with hatred in his eyes.

'I've been called out on this job,' he said, taking his eyes off me to look back over at the straggling passengers.

'No problem,' I said, lowering my placard. 'I don't have a car. We'll all go in your cab. I just came to meet him.'

'Out of my way, asshole,' said the cab driver without glancing at me.

'Out of my way, asshole.' This was a phrase which may not have corresponded exactly to habitual satire but nonetheless had a similar effect. Just rather more vulgar. If this man had a list of phrases on his bedside table, who would they be by? Julián Centella, Olivari, de la Púa?

I was about to explain to him that I didn't have the slightest interest in getting in his way, when I saw Eliás Traúm. A little cream-coloured hat—what was he doing with a hat, the heat was unbearable in Buenos Aires—greying sideburns, a five o'clock shadow from the plane, strong, slightly overweight, solid looking, all his teeth still, a decent-looking guy. He was looking over to the cab driver's placard and nodding his head.

He was coming over to us.

Later I realised I had been given a blow by an elbow.

His first movement was to grab my wrist when I tried to raise my placard in an attempt to greet Eliás. I was so taken aback by his fist crushing my hand that I dropped the placard and made no attempt to defend myself. And then as, somewhat disconcerted, I rubbed my freshly released wrist and bent to pick the placard up off the floor, there came that blow with the elbow. I got up slowly, staggering slightly. Two cab drivers were blocking my way. One of them was grinning. Obviously, Elías Traúm hadn't even seen me.

I managed to get to my feet and the two cab drivers moved away as if they had never come anywhere near me. Only then did I realise I had been hit. I was shaking. From fear. I was terrified. I didn't even look to see if it was still possible to catch up with Traúm. My mind was taken up with a single thought: I didn't want them to hit me again. I took a gulp of air and stood there. I passed my hand over my face and my mouth. There was no blood. But there was a bump on the right side of my forehead. Finally desperation overwhelmed me.

I had been hit and I had lost my passenger. Were they waiting for me at the entrance to finish me off? What had señor Pesce sent me into? I was having a very, very bad time of it. I hate this kind of thing.

For years I had managed not to interview anybody other than the odd, slightly suspect trade unionist, I never wrote a word that could impinge in any way on powerful people. Journalism was just a way of making a living: I would never do anything that meant taking chances.

I had thought of making a proposal to cover wars exclusively via satellites and robots. As far as I was concerned, risking your life to cover a war between, say, Peru and Ecuador, was as idiotic as the war itself. Was Pesce intent on ruining my strategy, my need for a healthy life? Had he set a trap to make me share the fate of those suicidal types back at the office who were capable of interviewing a serial killer in their own homes without even asking for a pay rise? Had Pesce's hatred materialised into concrete vengeance?

I wanted to tell myself, as I always do when something bad happens to me, 'the sky has fallen on top of my head,' which is the only thing the old Asterix tribal chief, Vitalstatistix, is afraid of.

But I had already discovered that when something really bad did happen to me, this was of no consolation at all.

When they invaded the narrow strip of land that separated me from barbarism, Asterix was a harmless little story and my life an inferno.

I had just one refuge where I could take shelter and keep a grip on common sense: Esther.

I found a one-peso coin in my pocket and ran to the phone.

'Esther,' I said, 'this is awful.'

'What's the matter?' she asked, alarmed.

The fright in her voice was a relief—it meant she wouldn't hang up on me.

By now she was used to me calling her up out of the blue, overcome by anxiety or terror. She would calm me down with just a few words, as you do a child. But since she left me she often put the phone down on me.

'I came to find some chap, for a piece I'm doing. A cab driver kidnapped him and whacked me with his elbow.'

'Where are you?' asked Esther, trying to keep her tone serious.

'At the airport, I came to find this guy for an interview, for the paper. But they took him away and hit me in the face.'

'Who took him away?'

'A cab driver, he elbowed me in the face.'

'Have you told the police?'

'No,' I said.

'Tell the police,' said Esther.

'I'm scared,' I said.

'Maybe he was nothing more than a cab driver,' said Esther. 'They can be violent. They'll fight for a passenger. Maybe he just wanted to steal your passenger. Maybe he thought you were a driver, too.'

'Yes, yes,' I said, grabbing on to this piece of logic for all I was worth. 'He must have wanted to get the fare. But he came to get him, too. He had a piece of paper with the same name on it.'

A boy had picked my placard up off the floor and was playing with it. He was waving the name of Elías Traúm in my ridiculous handwriting around in the air.

'Esther, I'm not sure I should tell the police. I'm going to wait a couple of hours and see what happens. Can I come and see you?'

Esther didn't answer.

'Esther?'

'Come on over,' she said.

I took a deep breath. I could still live, and stay sane. If Esther would see me, everything would go back to normal.

'What if they kill him?' I asked.

'Why should they kill him?' Esther tried to reason with me.

'I don't know. They hit me. What if they kill him?'

'Who is this man?'

'Nobody. Some guy who was going to tell me a story.'

'Is there any reason why somebody should want to kill him?'

'No, no reason. He's a Jew.'

'So?' asked Esther.

'I'm coming round to your house. Wait for me, please.'

'I'm here,' said Esther.

I hung up. The paper had given me the money for a cab, but I took the bus. From the desk where I bought my ticket I could see the boy still playing with the placard as if it were a balloon. I left him to it: maybe that was all that would be left of Elías Traúm.

Chapter four

Esther was looking lovely, as she always had since leaving me. She was wearing a dress of some flimsy material, and no bra. It was very hot, and a few tender drops of sweat, that I would swear were perfumed, were sliding gently down from her neck and disappearing between her breasts. Esther's breasts were lovely. I could never stand women with no breasts. Why had she left me? Why didn't she give herself to me? Why did she deprive me of the one happiness I had?

'Do you want tea?' she asked.

'Please,' I said.

'Hot or cold?'

'Hot first. I need to calm down.'

I followed her into the kitchen. She shouldn't have done it. A wave of melancholy seemed to drift out from the oven right through me. I couldn't bear it.

'Why did you leave me?' I asked her.

She dropped the tea bag into the cup. She looked at me as if I'd been putting her on, and all this desperation was just an excuse to go and talk to her.

'No,' I said before she could speak, 'they really did hit me. They kidnapped the man. But why did you leave me?'

'I'll tell you just once more,' said Esther, her voice grave and full, like her breasts. 'And if you go on talking about it, you'll go without your tea.'

I agreed silently, not moving a muscle.

'You deceived me,' said Esther.

I wasn't sure if she was referring to my sudden arrival at her house or the reason for our separation.

'I didn't deceive you,' I said.

'You went to bed with another woman.'

The accusation left a bitter taste in my mouth. My heart hurt. There are sexual relations a man brags about, and others which pursue him like shame for the rest of his life.

'We often said we wouldn't worry about a little fling outside our relationship,' I said.

'You never said that to me,' said Esther. 'I never heard you granting me the same privilege.'

'You said it to me,' I said.

'What I told you was that if anything like that happened without me knowing about it, it wouldn't worry me.'

'And yet you left me,' I ventured.

'I did know about it,' said Esther. 'And besides, she lives in the same building as me. I don't want to have a row with you, what's done is done. But what can I say—crazy? Fool?'

'Fool,' I chose. 'I can't live without you,' I added.

'I can't live with you,' said Esther.

'You know that woman doesn't interest me in the slightest,' I said. 'I despise her. I slept with her like a bad joke, precisely because I despised her…'

'Don't tell me again,' said Esther furiously, her tone black as dark wine. 'Stop telling me.'

'I'll never say it again,' I said.

We stayed silent until her anger passed.

'When I see you,' said Esther, 'I think of her. I think about that shitty old woman. When I meet her in the lift I think she's laughing at me. I'm going to move.'

'But...' I tried to interject.

'One more word and you're out of here.'

I wanted to say to her: 'Esther, I love you. I love you. I love you.'

But I was afraid these words would get me thrown out of the house. Esther is a serious woman, serious in love. Serious in the most marvellous pornography I have ever experienced with any woman. She is a biblical woman. She is a burning branch—her body always gives off warmth. I was capable of anything with her, everything in her seemed to me full of fruit and flavour. I could have eaten her. Beside her, I felt neither heat nor cold. I loved her sweat in the infernal summers and her gooseflesh in the worst winters. She had a virtue which kept me at her feet—her sexual fantasies always surprised me. And still I had done the most stupid thing in my entire life, sleeping with a fifty-year-old woman from the tenth floor.

Yes, I was a fool.

'What a woman says in bed is one thing,' Doctor Aguman, psychoanalyst and psychiatrist, had told me. 'But you shouldn't take it literally. We can't do the things we say in bed outside of it.'

Doctor Aguman was not my doctor. But he had revealed this truth to me late at a party. That was the difference between an adult and an individual with hopelessly childish writing.

'I can't sleep with you again,' said Esther, going back unexpectedly to the subject I wanted to avoid. Can't, I thought.

She handed me the tea. It was cold. I took out the bag and threw it into the rubbish, in the little orange bin. We went out of the kitchen and sat down in the facing armchairs in the sitting room.

'What happened?' she asked.

'The paper sent me to interview a man arriving today from Israel. His name is Elías Traúm. I'll tell you the whole thing later. The thing is, a cab driver appeared with a card just like mine (neater handwriting, I thought), looking for the same man. I went up to the cab driver and told him I was waiting for Traúm as well and that we should all come back together. Then he took the placard off me and elbowed me in the face.'

'You've got a bump,' said Esther. 'There, under the skin. Do you want some ice?'

'No. That whole thing about ice is just an old wives' tale,' I said.

Esther smiled. She smiled!

'It'll go purple,' she said. 'What are you going to do?'

'I don't know,' I said. 'I'm scared to go to the police. I don't want to get involved. I think I'll wait a couple of hours and then call Pesce at the paper. Let them deal with it.'

'Sounds reasonable,' said Esther.

She always managed to find the words that allowed me to live.

'I can't let them kill him.'

'Why should they kill him though?' asked Esther. 'What's he done?'

I was about to speak but she interrupted me. She placed a hand over my hand that was holding the cup of tea.

'Let's suppose the worst and they kill him. What's it got to do with you? Who is he? You've never spoken to him in your life. Any number of people get killed every day.'

'But I was supposed to meet him. And I got distracted.'

'When?' asked Esther.

'While I was waiting for him. I missed him.'

After a sip of tea I added:

'And he's a Jew.'

'So?' repeated Esther, just like before in the earpiece of the public phone at the airport.

Esther is more Jewish than I am. She celebrates Rosh Hashanah and Passover with their various prayers and foods, and she fasts for Yom Kippur. From the first time I met her, possessing such a woman had been my life's dream come true. The sexual passion of the woman of faith.

But she did not share my permanent suspicion as a hypothetical survivor of the Holocaust. For her the police are not necessarily Nazis. A 'Jew' was simply another person. A stranger like any unknown person in the street.

'I don't know,' I said. 'Besides, they'll fire me from the paper.'

'Just for that?' she asked.

'Absolutely,' I said. 'They'll fire me from the paper and I won't be able to pay you maintenance.'

Esther laughed aloud. I smiled too.

'If you like, I'll pay you maintenance,' I told her. 'Whatever you want.'

'There's no need,' said Esther, smiling.

We had not married either according to Jewish ritual or in the local register office, but for two years we had lived together like husband and wife.

'They won't throw you out for that,' said Esther. 'You haven't done anything wrong. Quite the opposite, I would have thought. It's the first time you've accepted a risky assignment, and anyway they mollycoddle you.'

'He didn't give me time to defend myself,' I said, slightly wounded in my virile pride. 'You know I was a warrior in the war between the Greeks and the Romans.'

'When you were twelve years old,' said Esther. 'Tell me who this Traúm is.'

'Have you heard of the three musketeers?' I asked her.

'A bit. Three Jewish lads. Three friends. Two of them disappeared. I heard something years ago, in eighty-three, I think, when democracy began.'

'When you were militant?'

'No,' said Esther. 'I heard it in a reunion of old comrades from the Hebrew Circle.'

Esther and I had both gone through the Hebrew Circle, but in those days we barely said hello to one another.

'Traúm was the third,' I said. 'Or, I don't know, the second, or the first. In any case, the only one to survive. The other two are dead. One of them was shot dead in the street, in Patricios Park. I don't know what strings the family pulled to get the body back. They found the other man's—'

'Stop,' said Esther. 'I get the idea. Don't tell me any more details. Go on.'

'There's not much else. There were three lads in the group. Three inseparable friends. They had started being active in the Jewish community when they were around fifteen, something like that. Three brilliant adolescents. Traúm and the others, I still don't know what their names were, went to the same high school. They really were extraordinary young men. Different groups and clubs used to get them to go and give talks.'

'What about?'

'About Zionism, modern Judaism, adapting scripture to the contemporary world.'

'Precocious boys.'

'Precocious Jewish boys, for sure. They brought out a couple of issues of a journal. It was called *God is silent.*'

'Were they rabid atheists?'

'No, they weren't rabid atheists but they managed to get militant atheists to buy their paper.'

'That won't have pleased the orthodox at all,' said Esther.

'They wouldn't look at it,' I replied. 'It was the name of God taken in vain.'

'And what was in the paper?'

'It was a typical adolescent thing. Essays, short stories, translated articles, places for dancing and dates. Oh, results of sporting events as well.'

'Did you find all this out for your interview?' asked Esther.

'No, I already knew about it. From the time I was in my lay period.'

'And later the three of them joined the Montoneros,' said Esther.

'Not Traúm,' I said. 'And the break was less dramatic than that. First of all one of them—what were their names now—started talking like a Marxist, saying the Jews had to join in the class struggle from where they were, going on about the Bund, and the Russian Revolution, and all that crap. Another one, Traúm I think, tried to rein him in with Zionist arguments. They would debate on the pages of the journal: "What had the Jewish Socialist struggle in Eastern Europe led to: some were murdered by their own comrades turned Nazi, and the rest were thrown into prison by Stalin.'"

'A lucid young man, this señor Traúm,' said Esther.

'I don't know if that was him. I suspect it was, since he went to live in Israel.'

'That doesn't prove anything,' said Esther. 'Lots of anti-Zionist Jews went to live in Israel to save their own lives.'

'But Traúm's face…I saw him today,' I said. 'I'm going to call the police.'

'Hold on,' said Esther. 'Calm down—think what you're going to say. Tell me everything first.'

'There's nothing else,' I said. 'Two of them joined the Montoneros and Traúm went to live in safety. Señor Pesce reckons all this is worth an article of a couple of hundred lines.'

'Seems to me it could be a book,' said Esther.

'Not one I'll write though,' I replied. 'I despise the Montoneros. And the only thing that interests me about Judaism is you.'

'And Israel,' said Esther.

'Do you want to come and live in Israel with me?' I asked suddenly.

Esther looked at me, her face pale.

'No,' she said. 'I don't want to live with you.'

I looked at her, for a long time. Why could I not stop looking at her?

Chapter five

When I reached home I was exhausted, what with Esther and being hit by the cab driver. I went into the bathroom and washed my face.

What was there to wash? I was a beaten man with a bump on his head. I lifted up my bangs and took a look at it. I was not alone—my bump was there with me.

Twenty-three years earlier, in a football championship match which River won, Boca's number five, Rógel, had shoved his elbow in the neck of River's number nine, Morete.

Two matches later River's coach, Ángel Labruna, sent River's number five—a kind of troglodyte called Merlo—to smash the face of Boca's number nine.

Rógel had been discreet and the referee couldn't send him off, while River lost their forward because of the blow. Merlo's thump, on the other hand, two meetings later, happened under the referee's nose and in the eye of the then limited number of television cameras allowed at the game. The whole country saw it.

Merlo was suspended for several games.

Everything I know about football comes down to River's

victorious campaign in 1975, but amongst the confusion of names and matches, my memory conserved above all Rógel's invisible elbow in Morete's neck.

The blow had knocked Morete out cold. Ever since then I couldn't stop wondering what it would be like to be on the end of it.

When I was a child, as I was drifting off to sleep, I often tried to imagine what it would be like to get a thump like that. I would bang my head gingerly against the wall in an attempt to see what the violence would be like so I could describe it.

Now I knew.

But why hadn't I checked the answering machine?

Ah, I had just been talking to Esther. If I normally hurtled into my house glaring at the unblinking red light of the answering machine it was because it might hold a message from Esther. Now that I had just been speaking to her, I couldn't give a damn about the machine's red light.

And this time the little red light had something to tell me. It was flashing like a bleeding star. Intermittent as the light of bad news. It winked mockingly at me—I've got some bad news for you.

I pressed the button.

It was señor Pesce. Traúm had turned up.

I pressed the pause button before Pesce went on talking.

I was sweating and my right hand was shaking.

'Traúm has turned up,' I thought, 'dead and naked by the side of the road. He's been partially scalped and had a swastika carved into his body.'

I pressed my hand on my face and with the other hand switched the cassette on again.

Pesce was saying that Traúm had called the paper and was in his hotel. He had had everything stolen: his bags and his clothes. They left him naked by the side of the road. He'd been lucky to reach his hotel, thanks to a police car that stopped when they saw him there with no clothes on. He was in the process of cancelling his credit card and ordering a new one. Under the circumstances…

Pesce's message finished here, and he hadn't thought it necessary to leave a second one.

It was seven in the evening. I called the paper.

After numerous rings Fabiana, the receptionist, answered, and when I asked for Pesce she dialled his extension. I was about to yell at her down the phone to please not dial any number and just get Pesce into reception and let me speak to him directly.

But I was too late: already my call was starting to wind its way around the erratic Milky Way of the interchanges, while a repulsive version of '*La cucaracha*', pipes and flutes and all, assaulted my hearing. I stuck it out for ten minutes.

I hung up and called again. This time switchboard answered and the electronic voice invited me to dial the extension, if I knew it. I did.

La cucaracha again, and finally Paco Gallé from the international desk answered.

'Is Pesce there?' I asked him.

'I'll put you through to him,' he said disdainfully.

La cucaracha.

Nobody answered. This time I decided to wait. I put the phone on to speakerphone.

After seventeen minutes Inés answered. Inés was the secretary to the boss of the political section.

'No, I don't know where Pesce is, do I? He's around somewhere. I'm sure I saw him around.'

She hung up, and so did I.

I dialled once more, and when the switchboard answered I decided to stay passive until the option 'you will be put through to an operator' was announced.

'This is the daily newspaper *El Presente*,' answered Fabiana in a singsong voice. 'How may I be of assistance to you?'

'Don't try and put me through,' I said. 'Hang on a minute. Is Pesce there, can you go and get him to the phone yourself?'

'Not a chance. He told me to give you the number of the hotel of someone or other. He says you're not to phone him until tomorrow evening. He's not sure he's going to let you write the piece.'

'Give it to me,' I said.

She gave me the number.

'Good,' I said. 'Now, can you go and get Pesce, please?'
'I'll put you through,' said Fabiana, and started dialling.
La cucaracha.

Chapter six

I hung up and immediately dialled the hotel. It was the Juncal Hotel, on Callao Avenue. An elegant hotel. Maybe señor Traúm was a man with money. I had been invited to parties and receptions in the rooms of the Juncal, and at the entrance I was always greeted by doormen with braided uniforms.

A receptionist answered, and I said I wished to speak to señor Traúm.

'What room number, please?'

I had forgotten to ask Fabiana which room number he had.

'He didn't tell me,' I said. 'I imagine he's just arrived. Elías Traúm.'

'Just a moment, please,' said the girl.

She was almost certainly working out whether to hang up there and then or check my phone number and get the police onto me. I might be one of the attackers, after all.

A new tune made itself heard in my ear. 'Tragedy', by the Bee Gees, in its full symphonic instrumental version.

A human voice replaced it. Maybe this was the hotel owner.

'Yes,' I said. 'I would like to speak to señor Traúm. I don't know his room number, but I am sure he's staying there with you. Elías Traúm.'

'Speaking,' said the voice.

'Elías?' I asked.

'Who is this?' he asked, a note of alarm in his voice.

'This is Javier Mossen!' I shouted, as if I were his cousin. 'I went to meet you at the airport.'

'Mossen?' he replied, still guardedly.

'The journalist. Señor Pesce sent me to meet you at the airport.'

'Oh,' he said, relieved. 'The journalist. What a business! They took everything. I was just trying to have a bit of a rest.'

'I see,' I said, 'I see. I just wanted to make sure you were all right. And to say how sorry I am for what happened. I was there, you know. I was standing there with a placard with your name on it.'

'Yes, I saw the card,' said Traúm, a trace of irony in his voice.

'No, you saw the cab driver's board. You didn't get to see mine.'

I didn't want to make him even more anxious by telling him how I had been elbowed in the face.

'Are you all right then?' I asked.

'I didn't expect anything different from my country,' he said, sounding cheerful for the first time. 'I expect I'll feel better after a bit of sleep.'

'Is there anything you need?' I asked.

'No. My card insurance will cover everything. My new card is on its way. I'll be fine.'

We were both silent. But neither of us hung up.

'Señor Traúm,' I said, 'to tell you the truth I was frightened. I can't tell you how glad I am to hear you are all right.'

'Thanks a lot. You've no need to worry. Don't forget I'm from Argentina, I'm not a raw tourist.'

'Shall we do this piece?' I asked, against my will.

'I don't know, really I don't. You know I just came to relax. It was Pesce who said maybe it was time to tell some of the story.'

'Pesce?' I said, knowing I should stop there. 'Do you know Pesce?'

'Of course. Otherwise how would you all have known that I was coming to Argentina? I'm hardly famous, am I?'

'Oh, right. I just wanted to say how pleased I am that you are fine. Before I go to sleep I'm going to say *Lehaim* for you.'

'Ah, you're one of us,' Traúm said to me.

'I try,' I said.

'*Hakol yehudim tovim*', said Traúm.

'I don't speak Hebrew.'

'We are all good Jews,' Elías translated for me. 'That's what Guidi's grandmother used to say. We took up the expression for ourselves. Every time we found ourselves in some emergency situation, or something awkward, one of the three of us would say, *Hakol yehudim tovim*.'

I didn't know what to say.

'Of course,' Traúm went on, 'it never made the slightest difference.'

'Did they just rob you?' I went on. 'How did they know your name?'

'I'd rather not think about it anymore. I'm only here a week. Thank God I don't live here. It's over now, nothing else will happen.'

'Of course,' I said. 'I'm sorry I bothered you.'

'No, no bother at all. The truth is I was worried all that business about the article was going to be a real hassle. But I didn't mind talking.'

'How long is it since you spoke Spanish, though?' I said, amazed. 'You speak it perfectly.'

'The thing is I only like Argentine girlfriends,' said Traúm. 'National flesh still has its attractions. And what with relatives, friends, mothers-in-law…I don't know when I last saw an Israeli.'

'I went to Jerusalem two years ago,' I said, apropos of nothing.

Why did I carry on talking? What sense was there in this conversation now that both of us were safe? His life was safe, I was safe from having to write the piece for the paper. I carried on talking because it was my way of thanking God who had given back the life of this man I did not know. We men have to talk because, as Traúm well knew, God is silent. And besides, this dialogue with a man who I considered to have been providentially torn from the teeth of tragedy was the only thing that stopped me wallowing in the memory of Esther.

'I'll be honest with you, señor Traúm,' I said. 'Since I was the one who was sent to pick you up, I felt responsible for what happened. I don't really care about the article. I didn't care about it much when I went to pick you up. But knowing you are safe and sound is the best thing that's happened to me in the last year.'

'Do you mean this year that's just started?' he asked, 'or the one that's just finished?'

'Both,' I said.

'Tell you what,' said Traúm. 'I'm not going to be able to sleep. I was trying to relax in front of the TV, but there isn't a single decent movie on. Do you drink whisky?'

'I do.'

'There's a small bar just near here.'

I almost shouted. I was there with the cordless phone. This was clearly a phrase from Bioy.

'I'm on my way,' I managed to say.

Chapter seven

During the taxi ride I thought about the fact that he had given me a first name: one of the musketeers was called Guidi. Guido, probably.

The doormen in their braid and epaulettes opened the door for me. But I had no luggage for them to help me with, or car to be parked, or tip to give them. They consoled themselves by pointing out the reception desk.

I asked for señor Traúm and the receptionist asked me for the room number.

'I haven't got it,' I said. 'But he's expecting me. Tell him Javier Mossen is here.'

'Wait there, please,' said the receptionist, pointing to a few padded chairs placed round a glass table piled high with various international magazines.

He didn't like my face.

'He's coming down,' said the receptionist.

I picked up a magazine about waterskiing, an American one. A buxom blonde was balancing on a small metal board while a bronzed young man sent her ploughing through the waves. She was wearing a one-piece swimming costume, blue, in which a round and play-ful rear end shifted peacefully and triumphantly. Would she let me sodomise her as we both skied on the water? Would the sea water irritate us?

Women in swimming costumes have always excited me. But in my childhood they were an obsession. I preferred leaning against the buttocks of a woman in a swimming costume to a naked one.

Traúm arrived. He took a look at the magazine. He took a look at me.

'In the States you only see them in magazines. Here they are walking the streets.'

'Señor Traúm,' I said, moved, 'you don't know how glad I am to see you.'

Traúm smiled.

I wanted to hug him, but that didn't seem appropriate. It was enough for me that he was alive and I could see him.

He put his hand on my shoulder.

'I'd forgotten that the evenings were so lovely here,' he said. 'I'll still buy you a whisky, but let's walk first.'

'With the greatest pleasure,' I said.

We went out on to Callao Avenue. The janitors greeted us defer-entially. Traúm replied with a nod of his head, and I did the same.

That's when I noticed he wore a skullcap.

He wore it hidden among the little dark hair he had left amidst a sea of grey. It was held in place with a clasp of buckled wire. It was black and borderless.

We were walking along Callao towards Santa Fe.

'Callao's so long!' he said.

I agreed.

He stopped and struck his forehead.

'What an idiot,' he said. 'What are we heading towards Santa Fe for? I want to see Ital Park!'

I looked at him sadly.

'What's the matter?' he asked.

'Ital Park,' I said.

'What's happened to Ital Park? Don't tell me they've put a bomb there as well?'

'No. They've taken it away,' I said. 'It's not there anymore.'

'Are they crazy? How can they take Ital Park away?'

'A girl was killed there a couple of years ago, on a ride called the Matterhorn. Her car flew off the wheel and the girl died.'

'That's awful,' said Traúm.

'Terrible,' I agreed. 'It coincided with the renewal of the Ital Park concession. And so it wasn't renewed.'

Traúm took the news in a worried silence that ended in a resigned smile.

'Well,' he said, 'let's head to Santa Fe then. What's there instead of Ital Park?' he asked, as we went over one of those short roads with long names which crisscrossed the classier part of Callao.

'A park,' I said.

'Is The Lighthouse still there?' he asked.

'The Lighthouse? The bar?'

'Yes, that bar called The Lighthouse. On Callao and Corrientes.'

'It's on Montevideo and Corrientes,' I corrected him. 'Yes, it's still there.'

'Montevideo? Are you sure? Next to a subway entrance, isn't it?'

'Yes. It's the exit for Uruguay stop. Maybe you are confused because there's one on Callao as well.'

'I could have sworn it was Callao. The Lighthouse. There's no subway in Jerusalem.'

'Do you live in Jerusalem?'

'Twenty-one years now.'

He looked at the sky and up along Callao, which seemed to stretch out endlessly.

'This isn't bad, is it?' he asked.

'I don't think so, no,' I said.

I raised a silent prayer of thanks to God that I could enjoy the warm night air without the memory of Esther reducing me to tears.

'On Callao and Corrientes,' said Traúm, 'sorry, on Montevideo and Corrientes, Guidi saved Benjamín's life.'

'He was called Benjamín?' I asked.

'Benjamín,' repeated Traúm. 'I don't suppose you'll believe me. He was a couple of months younger than Guidi, and the smartest of the three of us.'

How could he be called Benjamín? Someone called Benjamín can't get into the Montoneros. He can't sing idiotic songs at the top of his voice, and brandish guns about, and say he'll kill so and so and make a stairway out of the bones of such and such. No. A person called Benjamín has to be protected by his name, he can't be riddled with bullets in Patricios Park, his...his bones? No, it was impossible. And God is silent.

'Benjamín joined some socialist group or another,' said Traúm. 'Can you believe it, I can't remember what it was called? They were Trotskyite, that much I remember. Can you think of anything more like a rabbi than a Trotskyite? Trotsky was a mentally defective rabbi. Or a confused rabbi, if you prefer. A crazy rabbi. Trotsky. The flower of anti-Semitism. Trotsky, backsliding Jew. Don't you think the Trotskyites are like a Jewish sect?'

'No. The Trotskyites are more religious,' I said.

Traúm laughed.

'Trotsky,' he went on. 'How did he get to be such a rabbinical schmuck? He was drooling. A mental retard, with all due respect. "Miss, miss, Stalin hit me." "I desire the good of all humanity, with the exception of my relatives." "Miss, miss, Stalin hit me." And he was the one who had put weapons into the hands of the Red Army, the miserable bastard.'

'Tell me about Benjamín,' I asked him.

'What do you want me to tell you,' said Elías, still furious, totally losing the thread of his story.

'What you were going to tell me.'

'Guidi saved Benjamín's life. On Callao and Corrientes.'

I didn't correct him.

'Benjamín was in this Trotskyite sect. PST, TPS, STP, whichever it was. All mental retards. And Benjamín kept up a heated discussion

with Guidi: no weapons, said Benjamín. No weapons. The working
class has its own form of struggle: strikes, demonstrations, delegates.
Benjamín hadn't joined the Montoneros. And Guidi said to him:
they're going to kill them like flies. You've read a lot of Mahatma
Gandhi. They're going to mow them down like flies. We have to get
organised like an army, we have to learn to shoot. And the masses?
said Benjamín. The masses are not an army. I'm with the masses.
The destiny of the masses is my destiny. They'll kill you both, Guidi
would say to him, you and the masses. Can you explain to me how
two young Jewish men, two intelligent young men, could talk such
rubbish?'

'What about you?' I asked him.

'Hang on and I'll tell you,' he said, evading my question and
using a familiar form of address at one and the same time. 'Benjamín
was on a trade union list that was opposed, just for a change, to the
official list. The official list had won by a big majority. But Benjamín
said that "the masses" followed his line. Who are the masses? Why
don't they ever vote for the "masses" list? Well, the leadership, let's
call them the Blues—are they still called by colour?—had reached
an agreement with the bosses' organisations. If I remember rightly it
was the Plastics union.'

Traúm laughed.

I didn't ask what he was laughing at. But he told me anyway.

'Can you imagine a young Jew, intellectual, with rabbis for
forebears, as a militant in the Plastics union? No, the Left is a virus
which gnaws away at intelligence. How else can you explain it? The
Blues had come to a very favourable agreement, I don't remember
what it was. Some extra back pay, or pay to keep in line with the
cost of living. And something about holidays. I remember there was
something about holidays.'

Traúm was totally at ease with all the trade union terminology,
more than I am when writing about it. I could imagine him listening with boredom and distaste to his two friends who'd suddenly got
caught up in a whirlwind of impatience and madness.

'What did Benjamín do?' said Traúm, with the classic intona-
tion of rabbis when they ask their pupils a rhetorical question about

a key figure in the Torah. 'Together with his handful of revolutionary comrades he organised a demonstration against the agreement. Gains were not to be asked for but fought for, he said. Pay rise? A joke. Holidays? Let the bosses go and do the work. I can't remember now exactly what their demands were. I can remember faces, I can see everything, but I can't say what they were wanting.'

Along Callao we had gone through Santa Fe, and we were on one of the pavements in Paraguay. Opposite us, half deserted, the enormous square that stretches to Rodríguez Peña and Marcelo T. de Alvear appeared, like an oasis. By silent agreement we sat down on a wooden bench whose paint was peeling off. One of the seat planks was missing and some of the screws were poking out, but at least there was no spit or anything even worse all over it.

Traúm looked at the bench and stroked the wood.

'Benjamín and his sect decided to go out to "denounce" the agreement with a march. A nighttime march from the Obelisk to Callao and Corrientes. Ah, that's why I got confused. It was Callao and Corrientes. A short but serious march, that's how he saw it. "We're going to mobilise all the different groups."

'Imagine it—a march against an agreement that the majority of the workers were happy with. No. You can't imagine it. Nobody was going to go. Nobody except Benjamín and his zealots. And the thugs from the Blues, of course. Why wouldn't they go? It was nighttime, a bit fresh out, they'd already eaten and had a bit of time with the wife. "Let's go and give the buggars a good thumping, and for dessert we'll have ourselves a Jew." It really was an entertainment not to be missed.

'Guidi said to him that leading a march like that was suicide. But to go unarmed is the suicide of an idiot. "You have to go armed," he said, "you and anybody going with you." "The strength of the working class has no need of arms," Benjamín told him, or something like that. "There's no chance of a clash: we're going to be an overwhelming majority. Because it's not just the plastic workers, lots of others will be joining us."

'I can still remember the way he put it—plastic workers.

'Guidi insisted, and begged him to arm at least a couple of his men. He even managed to drag some sort of coherent response out of him. Benjamín said, "We'll be marching right along Corrientes Avenue. They wouldn't dare try to beat us up in the middle of the street, under the eye of the whole world."

'"Benjamín," said Guidi, "they kill people in the light of day, in a taxi. Does it seem to you beyond the bounds of possibility that they could whip up a fake fight and take advantage of the chaos to kill you?"

'Neither Guidi nor Benjamín ever used expressions such as "smash your head in,"' Traúm broke off to say. 'They kept a semblance of dignity. At least they called death what it was, death. And Guidi said to him, "they'll take advantage of the chaos to kill you." Not "to smash your head in."

'The day, the night of the march arrived. Benjamín set off from the Obelisk with a huge red flag which said, *No to the traitors' agreement*. And below that it said, *For a workers' agreement*.

'It was a cold night, towards the end of August 1974. People were in the bars, as usual, but the street was unusually empty. How many men do you think went on the march Benjamín organised?'

'I don't know,' I replied.

'Twelve,' replied Traúm. 'Twelve people. They were like the apostles. There were the eleven people who had organised it, plus the girlfriend of one of them. A cute little thing with a big arse, who brought a note of realism to this ragtag collection of madmen. They set off towards Uruguay. I followed them from the pavement. I was looking at the girl. You only find arses like that in Argentina.'

I agreed enthusiastically and asked:

'What about you? What were you doing there?'

'I went to keep an eye on Benjamín. It was one of the last times I stuck my neck out. I wanted to make sure he got home that night. Or at least I wanted to say good-bye to him. Or die with him.'

'Why didn't you join the march?'

'Not in a million years!' said Traúm angrily. 'I was prepared to die with him, but not to back him up in his stupid ideas. When they reached Uruguay a group of twenty people came out of the subway entrance. I counted them one by one. They were in a group. They were frightening. Some were wearing sweatsuits and others had leather jackets. These were the thugs sent by the Blues, no doubt about that. They watched the march with a mixture of amusement and hunger. They wanted to hit. They wanted to kill. And these people didn't believe in the "power of the majority": they were all armed.

'I looked at Benjamín's face. He didn't see me. But he looked nervous. And I knew he was thinking that maybe he'd made a mistake. I knew the expression on his face when he was beating himself up over some mistake he'd made.

'Maybe I'm not telling you the story properly. Let me start again. The twelve of them came from the direction of the Obelisk singing. They were singing a song that…'

Traúm pinched his nose between his fingers, the classic and useless gesture people from Buenos Aires make when they are trying to remember something.

'How did it go now…' he mumbled.

And then, triumphantly:

'I know, I know!'

He started to sing in an extraordinary voice, a kind of tuneless growl, as if he was intoning a *kol nidre*, the traditional Jewish prayer said for Yom Kippur.

A truck for the garbage
And an arm to do the work
With the union of the comrades
Who have laid an egg
We will be victorious.

'That's what they sang. They came down Corrientes singing that. When they sang it seemed as though there were more of them. But there were twelve of them, including the chick with the big arse.

'When they get to Uruguay, they see them. A flock of lambs thrown to the wolves. The time when they will lie down together hasn't arrived yet. The dozen out-of-tune men with their open shirts spot the twenty or so hulks with their sweatsuits and leather jackets.

They stood there. They stopped singing. One of the lads, the boy-friend I suppose, gave the girl a warning tap on the shoulder and I saw her set off quickly back in the direction they had come from, towards the Obelisk. Thank God they let her go.

'I would have headed off after the girl without a second thought,' said Traúm. 'Benjamín should have gone right behind her. But he stood there, and so did I. In the middle of Corrientes, in the middle of the silence, with twenty thugs closing in on a dozen unarmed wretches.

'They weren't going to kill all of them. But they would all get a beating, a bad beating with sticks and metal poles, and they would kill one or two. If they killed just one of them it would be Benjamín. If they killed two, it would be Benjamín and another one.

'Finally Benjamín understood they were going to be killed, right there in the middle of Corrientes.

'And so…' Traúm fell silent. He was playing with me. Creating suspense. For the hundredth time he looked up at the sky. What was he looking for?

'Would you have gone back with the girl?' he asked me.

'Without a second thought,' I said. But I doubted it.

'What an arse she had,' he said.

'And then?' I urged him to go on.

'And then the waters of the Red Sea broke, and the sea swallowed up the Egyptians, and God saved his people. But why did he save them just the once?'

'What happened then, Elías?'

'Then, from the mouth of the subway station, Guidi came out. Guidi and around fifty people. Too many to count. From both the subway exits on opposite sides of the street. Some of them were carrying sticks and others wore black bracelets. I suspect all of them were armed. These people realise the other lot are armed. Guidi and his men came out of the subway entrance singing, loud and clear:

A truck for the garbage
And an arm to do the work
With the union of the comrades

*Who have laid an egg
We will be victorious.*

The whole group, around fifty or so of them, headed straight towards the Blues' twenty thugs, singing that stuff about the truck and the garbage.

The whole scene was like an epiphany. The twenty boys from the Blues stood there, frozen to the spot for a brief moment of utter surprise and then, as if they had heard one of those dog whistles that humans can't hear, slowly, one by one, they started singing, "A truuuuuck for the gaaaaarbage". They joined in the demonstration singing at the tops of their voices until they reached Callao. And there they broke up in orderly fashion.'

'Don't write that, please,' said Traúm, as I was laughing at the end of the story.

'Why not?' I asked.

'No, don't write that. That's a story I'll give to you. Don't tell it. It makes no sense. Now the two of them are dead. It would betray them to tell people this story to make them laugh.'

'If you don't want me to write it, I won't write it,' I said.

'Don't write it,' he said again. 'Two weeks later Benjamín went over to the Montoneros.'

'I see,' I said. 'To the same cell as Guidi?'

'No.'

He looked at the sky for the hundredth and first time.

'I'm very tired,' he said. 'I didn't get any sleep. I never sleep on the plane. And the assault did nothing to relax me.'

'Was it very bad?' I asked.

'A gun. Hand everything over, including your clothes. I'm very rational in these moments. Take everything you want, lads. But there's something else.'

'I thought as much,' I said. 'They had a card with your name. What else?'

'They told me to keep quiet.'

'About what?'

'All this, I guess, everything I'm telling you about. There's no other possible motive. I suppose they knew I was going to do an article.'

'It can't be that,' I said. 'Every Sunday the papers and magazines carry articles of the sort I was going to do on you. Nobody gets killed for that, it's ancient history.'

'There's no ancient history, and people can be killed for anything. But they're not going to kill me for that, don't worry. But I need to get back to the hotel.'

'Of course,' I said, 'let's stay in touch, though. I'll just ask one thing of you,' I added.

'Tell me.'

'Allow me to take you back to the hotel in a taxi.'

Elías Traúm accepted and I saw him go up the steps into his elegant hotel, guarded by the doorkeepers. I couldn't have slept without knowing he was back safe and sound in his room. I sighed. The rest of his life was his own problem.

I had stayed in the taxi, and I gave him the address of my house.

Two men standing on a corner opposite the Juncal Hotel watched as I left. One of them took a cigarette out of his mouth.

Chapter eight

I reached home sweating and with a tic in my right eye. My bump was hurting me, too. Luckily, even in the depths of my despair it occurred to me that Traúm either hadn't noticed it or he had noticed and hadn't mentioned it. I felt like a boy who doesn't want to worry his father.

But those two men had stared at me. And they were standing opposite the hotel. Was this one of my recurrent paranoias? No. The evidence was clear: they looked like hired killers, they were standing opposite the hotel, and they were staring at me.

They were following us. Me? Why? Because I had gone to meet Traúm. Because I had gone out for a walk with Traúm, and because I had dropped Traúm off at his hotel.

My new place, an apartment with one room, kitchen and bathroom, which I shared with a sad mess, was emptier than if I had never been in it. The tap was dripping, and out of the window, over terraces and neighbouring dark apartments, I could make out the deserted Calle Pringles, awash with ill omen. I was sweating more and more, and my eye was doing as it pleased. My stomach was making ridiculous noises, and my heart was racing.

I reckoned a coffee would calm me down. The coffee touched something in my brain, and for a moment I thought I was going mad. I looked at my watch: it was two o'clock in the morning and I was thinking of killing myself.

I ran to the bedside table and stared at the written phrases.

As long as I read, something inside me seemed to restore itself to some sort of equilibrium. But as soon as I looked away the vertigo swept over me again. I was dripping with sweat. My hands were wet.

I called Esther.

I knew that she would allow this. I was going to suggest going back to her house, I just wanted her to listen. She would grant me that. She wouldn't call the police because I was calling her at two-thirty in the morning, and she wouldn't hang up.

As I dialled I asked God just one thing—that she wasn't with another man. I could accept that she was asleep and that the answering machine would take my call. But not if she answered me with that cautious voice of a woman with a man by her side.

She answered and I regretted calling her. I would have preferred it if the machine had answered. Now how could I tell if in what had been our bed there wasn't a man hoping it would be a brief conversation, asking her with gestures who it was, while she replied in her turn with signs and gestures that it was nobody important, a sick relative.

'Hallo,' she said.

Her voice sounded sure and sleepy, sleepy because of the time it was, sure that it was me.

I replied immediately; as much as I feared a man next to her in bed, I couldn't risk any telephone silence at two thirty in the morning, like a dangerous lunatic.

'Esther, it's me,' I said.

'I know,' she said.

'I've ruined my life, Esther, I've ruined my life. There are two men after me. It's not paranoia. They're following me, honestly. They're following Traúm. But they're following me. I've ruined my life, Esther. You know I hate these things, I've always avoided them. I've ruined my life, and I'm terrified.'

'Tell me what happened.'

'I just saw them looking at me. They were waiting outside Traúm's hotel. Maybe they were waiting for him.'

'What's he thinking of doing?'

'Traúm? Nothing. Going back to Israel. He's not afraid for his life.'

'Do you want to come here and sleep on the sofa?' Esther asked me.

'I'd like to, but I can't. I can't take them to your house, if they're following me. I shouldn't even have called you. What if they've tapped my phone?'

'Don't worry. But you're going to have to do something. Don't you want to call the police?'

'No. First thing tomorrow I'll talk to Pesce. I'm going to sleep at the office.'

Esther laughed.

'Esther,' I said, 'I swear that if I get out of this I'll become a good man.'

'You'll get out of it,' said Esther, 'I'm sure of that.'

'But what does it mean, to be a good man?'

Esther didn't answer.

'Now I'm glad I'm not living with you,' I said sincerely. 'That way I don't cause you any trouble.'

'I'm not going to be able to sleep now anyway,' said Esther.

'You're still worried about me,' I said.

'Call me in the morning.'

I was about to ask her, 'Are you alone?'

But I said:

'Goodnight, darling.'

'Goodnight, try and sleep.'

And she hung up.

I went to look at myself in the mirror. My eye was twitching a little less but the bump looked bigger. I felt a churning in my stomach but nothing happened. Amongst my books I found *The War of the Jews* by Flavius Josephus. I put the kettle on the stove and settled down to a sleepless night.

Chapter nine

My cubicle was in the fortress of Masada. Down below, Tito and his army—a large part of the world population—were waiting to annihilate me. As long as I stayed awake, my fortress of an apartment would protect me. But if I fell asleep, I would never wake up again.

It didn't matter what era we were in, as far as I was concerned it was always the age of the assassins.

My watch seemed stuck at three in the morning. I knew that if I made it through to four o'clock, I would survive. The light of day would mean I could make decisions and plan a worthwhile flight. The very air was standing guard.

I forced myself not to look at my watch, trying to convince myself that was the only way the hands would move round. Time passes only when we are not watching.

And indeed, when I looked again, it was just past four o'clock in the morning. I'd added a few coffee grains to the mate tea, but there was no need—my insomnia was guaranteed. At four thirty I felt the onset of weariness felt by a man who cannot sleep. Everything around me disgusted me, as I suffered the irritating sensitivity that inevitably follows from not distancing oneself from the world for the obligatory eight hours.

I dropped onto my bed and fell asleep.

I woke at eight, and as my vision was still blurred from sleep I thought I saw the door open. I gave a yelp of fright and prepared to die without defending myself. But it was only a trick of the eye, the daytime residue of a nightmare.

I couldn't drink any mate tea or coffee. I went down to the bar on the corner and asked for an orange juice. I stopped myself looking out of the window and fixed my eyes on a copy of the newspaper I worked for. It must have been a month or so since I had actually read it.

From the bar doorway I flagged down a taxi and headed over to the office.

Fabiana greeted me with her mouth puckered and an anxious look on her face. I had never had much chance to see her arse, hidden as it was behind the rigid reception desk. But the thickness of her lips pointed to a full body with little subtlety about it. She must have had the rear end of an untamed mare, or at least dominated only by the higher authorities at the newspaper. Whatever, I was sure she would only let herself be sodomised against her will, that that was how she bestowed all her sexual favours, needing to be pulled by her hair or cornered like a tigress. There was no moment in my life in which I felt a weakness for battles that might include the possibility of defeat.

'You're early,' she said.

'Is Pesce here?' I asked her.

Pesce's office, no paradoxes here, was like a fish bowl, just as his name meant fish. A glass box where he could always be seen with his face behind some paper of the previous few days. His computer screen had a depressing screen saver, a face that was a combination of Chaplin and Gardel, with a hat that was a mix of both of theirs, and a stick that shook like Chaplin's in *The Kid* or like Gardel's in the poster for the pizzeria 'The Immortals'. In black and white, the dreadful face sat there winking at the user.

I went in without knocking and Pesce looked at me without a word.

He looked back to his paper as if pretending he still had a line left to read, and finally he looked back at me with a fake questioning expression, as if he didn't know the reason for my abrupt entrance.

'They're following us, Pesce,' I said, unsure whether to use the familiar or more formal mode of address, but keeping the 'señor'. 'Me and Traúm.'

I was on the point of blurting out: *Can you tell me what the fuck is going on?*

But I was afraid of scaring him.

'Can you tell me what is going on?'

Pesce didn't change the position of his face. But imperceptibly his eyes shifted from pretend alarm to accepting that we both knew what we were talking about.

'I'll be short and to the point, Mossen,' Pesce said to me. 'Unlike a good proportion of the people who work in this place, the only thing that concerns you is your safety. I'm aware of that. You'd rather count the number of names in the phone directory than get anywhere near a space rocket or cover the lead up to a war. You'd even refuse to cover the Napoleonic campaign—you'd refuse to travel in time, if that meant there was the slightest risk.'

'It's just that I do features,' I said, noting that the conversation was taking a favourable turn.

'I made a mistake,' Pesce went on. 'A big mistake. I should never have given you this piece. Not that I could have known. The journalist who gave me the information about Traúm is well on with the thing now and you can drop it.'

'You can tell me his name then,' I said jovially.

'Now less than ever,' Pesce answered seriously.

'And will you let those people following me know that it's nothing to do with me anymore?' I asked ironically.

'They already know,' he said, still seriously.

This time, the look of real astonishment and slight fear was in my eyes.

'Unlike you, Mossen, I am a journalist,' said Pesce. 'I know the rules of the game. I know which cards have to be put on the table to bet hard and which you have to hold back to keep your bet safe. In this case I might say I was already getting my money back. But you are the card I am keeping back, Mossen. You don't need to speak to Traúm again. Nobody's going to fuck with him, they won't even look at him; but don't get it into your head to speak to Traúm again, either by phone or in person. And don't ask me anything else. You want safety? You're just as safe as you were before I made the stupid error of entrusting you with this article. You never took work home with you: on occasion this caused us practical difficulties but never serious spiritual problems. Stick to your usual line.'

'What happened, Pesce?' I couldn't help blurting out, almost looking for some kind of complicity and forgetting all sense of irony.

'I'll tell you just the once. Just the once. Any more questions and you'll be out of here. One more question and I won't be responsible for you anymore.'

Pesce paused for a moment and glanced down at the old paper on his desk. Then he said:

'I thought it was one story and in fact it was another.'

Chapter ten

Almost all good jokes about paranoid people converge on a single, serious doubt. Is paranoia a state of alienation which imagines dangers where there are none, or a state of lucidity which perceives real dangers invisible to everyone else?

All paranoid people who are not psychotic will claim the second explanation; the wives of paranoids will go for the first.

But whether it's because of their excessive lucidity or their infirm imagination, paranoids have a bad time of it.

My state of mind after my chat with Pesce, despite all his reassurances as to my personal safety, was a whirlwind of agitation and desire to take flight to places that didn't even exist. I was afraid for Traúm. Fear for my own safety had mutated into fear for the safety of Traúm.

I hadn't asked Pesce, and it didn't seem appropriate to do so, if the killers would leave Traúm in peace as well. Now I regretted not asking the question.

'You could still call him on the phone,' I said to myself, 'and tell him you want to ask one last question.'

'No more questions,' I answered myself, 'he said no more

questions. Do you want to live? No more questions. If you want to do something different, then ask away.'

But I wanted to live. I wanted to live with Esther. And without Esther I didn't want to live.

I couldn't call her. I knew she was edging towards the point where the desperate tone of my calls, which up to now had elicited a tender response, would start to get on her nerves.

Other times Esther's patience had seemed to me to be endless.

That was why I had lost her.

I'd first seen the neighbour from the tenth floor at a residents' meeting.

She was a florid old witch, red-haired and loud-mouthed.

She was fifty years old and moaned about everything. She wanted to sack the building's administrators, and accused the other residents of all being thieves. She was looking for support from me.

In the downstairs room where the neighbours would meet to waste their time and lose their tempers—and which I once found myself obliged to go to 'so that the sky would not fall on my head'— she was shaking her body in time with her yells, and two wrinkly but lively, light-coloured breasts with their large nipples were competing for the right to jump out of her bra, just as Jacob and Esau fought in their mother's womb.

And then I wanted all the other neighbours to disappear, and while she carried on yelling in her obsessive and aggressive manner, to grab her by the hips. I wanted to take hold of her aged breasts and squeeze them hard while I thrust myself impudently into her buttocks, amidst sweat and filth. In that downstairs room.

But I knew it was impossible. I knew it was dangerous. I knew it was absolutely the wrong thing to do.

She was a madwoman with an empty arsehole. A machine of aggressive energy that had to be contained in her rear exit. Who would act as rudder to this ship of adulterous fury?

Not me. It couldn't be me. I was virtually married, I was happy. If the world was not exactly smiling upon me, at least it was not blinding me. I had found my hiding place. Esther loved me.

Delia—for that was her name—gave me no reason to stop thinking about her. Wherever I happened to bump into her—in the elevator, on the ground floor, in the square or the supermarket—she asked for support in her crusade against our administrators and the neighbours in general. Only if all the neighbours got together could we give the administration what it deserved; and only in a dual entity of solid principles, of which I was without doubt a large part, could we give the rest of the neighbours what they deserved. It didn't escape my notice that in agreeing with one or another neighbour I passed swiftly over the legion of neighbours to be fought against. But all I could hear amidst her inflamed declarations were vulgar pleadings:

'I need someone to fuck me in the arse, I need someone to fuck me in the arse.'

I was compelled to attend a second residents' meeting. An apartment on the third floor had been burgled, and we neighbours had to come to some sort of agreement: either we resigned ourselves to leaving things as they were and putting up with a burglary now and then, or else we looked for another expensive solution and all resigned ourselves to a different kind of theft.

We voted for both motions: this was one of those rare occasions when logic allows you to choose two opposite alternatives at the same time.

There was a row anyway. The purpose of residents' meetings is to allow us to express our hatred at this daily business of living together: agreements and decisions are nothing more than a mere excuse.

Delia, of course, threw herself into the fray. She insulted the administrator—accusing him of favouring one of her female neighbours, for mysterious reasons—and refused to apologise even when a young man from one of the other flats, who up to then had seemed to be her staunch ally, urged her to.

When Delia refused to apologise to the administrator the young man reacted suddenly and impulsively, jumping up, screaming in the face of the red-haired amazon and exiting the room.

It wasn't entirely clear to me if the young man was Delia's boyfriend or the administrator's. The only dealings I'd had with him were to ask which floor he was going to when we got into the elevator together.

Anyway, his shouting had the most extraordinary result: Delia shut up.

Her face, normally so twisted and agitated, looked like that of a child caught out in mischief; her mouth curled into a slightly shamed smile; she looked down at the floor.

I didn't know how or when, but the words of a young man who had suddenly turned violent had given off the incomprehensible aroma of passion.

A couple of mornings later I met Delia in the foyer, and as we went up in the elevator she begged me to go back to her apartment with her. She was alarmed, afraid. Something terrible had happened.

Without consciously deciding to do so, driven by the power of her fear, I followed her. She let me into her apartment.

It was a mess. Piles of paper were dumped onto a large and ugly table. She took me over to the balcony.

She pointed to the balcony floor. She held her nose and pretended to start crying. She ran back into the sitting room and the unpleasant table covered with paper.

On the balcony floor, something was written with what looked like brick dust in scrawled writing:

'Great sucking, bitch!'

I hadn't yet taken in the mixture of praise and insult when Delia was back beside me. Her breathing was shallow and she was afraid. She had a piece of paper in her hand.

'This is the letter from Darío,' she said, showing me a signature on a circular she had sent round herself demanding that all the fire extinguishers on every floor be removed. 'This is the same handwriting as Darío's—it was Darío!'

Delia was waving the piece of paper around so much it was impossible to compare the handwriting, but for the few seconds I could look at them clearly—the shameless graffiti and the illegible signature—it could not have been clearer that they had, indeed, been written by the same hand.

Darío, of course, was the young man who had left her speechless by yelling at her. If we were to be guided by the improvised text Delia attributed to him, we might deduce that he had left her silent in more ways than one.

I didn't dare ask for clarification. But everything seemed to point to the fact that Delia was accusing Darío of breaking into her house and writing that filth on her balcony.

My deficient journalist's vocation might raise some doubts: had Darío already visited the flat with an excuse neighbourly or otherwise, with the complete consent of its owner, and was he now taking the delight of both as object of revenge? And what was he revenging himself for?

Neither of these enigmas offered a solution.

Delia opened her eyes wide with the fear of someone who has seen a monster, closed them with the feebleness of someone who suffers more than they can bear, rolled up the sleeves of her silk blouse and said:

'I've got gooseflesh. Touch my skin, look, here. I've got gooseflesh.'

And then, just a few steps away from the balcony and not far enough that people in the street couldn't see us, with her under the horrible table and me leaning against it, finally I lost myself.

Everything was certain. Her breasts were wrinkled but held the magical consistency of sexual hatred, her waist was flabby but moved swiftly in its greed; and the rest was a perversion, so hollow that any man would have felt himself a hero if he had been able to satisfy it.

Everything was certain, including hell.

I told Esther.

Chapter eleven

I went back to Paraguay Square—if you left the newspaper office and started walking you ended up there almost without noticing—and stopped to think. I couldn't call Esther. Pesce had forbidden me to call Traúm. Just the night before we had been sitting on this same bench and life had seemed possible for both of us. Now I hadn't slept and I could see a cloud of tragedy gathering over his head.

I had to call him, there was no choice.

If I called him from a public phone box nobody would be able to find out about it. What about the receptionist? What if his phone was tapped? What if my phone call put him in danger? Silence was better than that.

What if everything would be all right as long as I didn't contact him, and my call precipitated disaster?

I couldn't remember the hotel phone number and I took that as a clear sign that I shouldn't call.

Even so, I crossed over to a small bar on the last corner between Callao and Santa Fe, asked for a copy of the yellow pages and wrote down the phone number of the hotel.

Señor Traúm was not in his room. Did I wish to leave him a message?

No, thank you very much.

From a table pushed right up against the toilet a homosexual was staring at me unblinkingly.

At least, I thought, nobody's sent him to stare at me.

Chapter twelve

I'd stood a long time with the phone in my hand, looking down at where the money went in, and I was afraid the homosexual would see this as a tacit acceptance of his insistent gaze. When I came out of the phone box he winked at me and called the waiter over to pay.

I took a taxi.

I gave him the address of my house.

Finally, I said to myself, the sky had fallen down onto my head.

The receptionist knew my voice.

If—whoever it was who was watching Traúm—had the receptionist in his grasp, at that moment the wheel of misfortune had begun to turn.

They don't kill people for that, I told myself in the taxi. Every day in the paper, on the t.v., there were stories about the Montoneros, about torturers, assassins, victims. And these stories don't get people killed.

Traúm answered in my silent voice: *They kill people for anything. History is never over.*

I reached the entrance to my block.

As I went up in the elevator, I thought there was no solution. They would kill Traúm because of me and then I would have to find some way to die.

Maybe I could go to live in Bolivia and change my name. Transform myself into a slave or a slave owner. Forget all about myself.

I couldn't go and live in Israel after letting them kill Traúm.

I also ran the risk of running into some of his relatives or friends, who would come and wave their fists in my face.

I went in and felt the need for alcohol or tobacco. I had stopped smoking, my icebox wasn't working, and I didn't feel like going out again.

The answering machine was blinking.

'Esther!' I cried.

And I pressed 'play.'

It was my mother.

I listened without paying attention, until I realised what she was saying:

'...we're here having tea with señor Traúm, who knows Aunt Shula. Call me if you get this message.'

I lifted up the phone as if my mother's voice suggested she was still at the other end of the phone. But the electronic voice of the answering machine—while I was dialling my mother's number—announced that the call had been recorded ten minutes before.

My mother answered and I shouted at her.

'Is he still there?'

'He's here,' my mother said cheerfully. 'Are you coming over?'

'Yes. How did he turn up at your house?'

My mother laughed.

'It's quite a story...come on over and we'll tell you.'

'Let me speak to him,' I asked her.

She passed him to me.

'You have to go back to Israel, Elías,' I said.

'Of course,' he said. 'I'm only here for a visit.'

'I mean you have to go back tomorrow. Or today. Change your flight and leave.'

'Not that fast, no,' he said. 'I can't.'

'Ask the consulate for help.'

'There's no need,' he said.

'Elías, this isn't a joke,' I said. 'You told me yourself that they kill people for anything.'

'All the more reason,' said Elías, 'not to get worked up.'

He was making me furious.

'What are you doing there in my mother's house?' I asked, unable to become really angry.

'It's quite a story...' he said, handing me back to my mother. 'Come on over and we'll tell you.'

'They are going to kill my mother. They are going to kill my mother,' I thought in the elevator, 'they're going to kill my mother and it's my fault.'

What was Elías Traúm doing in my mother's house?

Chapter thirteen

My mother doesn't live in the heart of the Once district of Buenos Aires, but in an important artery of it. Although I love the whole area, these blocks depress me. It's Tucumán street up to Callao towards the gentile side, and down to Pueyrredón towards the Jewish end. Opposite the street where my mother lives half a dozen low-class porno cinemas have opened up. A bread shop of even less distinction has just about survived. And in the block itself was an orthopaedics shop, whose quality contributed nothing towards the improvement of its surroundings.

I arrived in time to prevent an unacceptable romance between my mother—chastely widowed for ten years and still a young fifty-five—and a clueless señor Traúm, whose sexual impulses did not waver even under the grimmest of circumstances. I remembered his musings over the butt of the girl on that pathetic march, despite the fact that they were about to bash his friend's head in.

They were both drinking tea and eating buffalo mozzarella at the enormous table in the sitting room. Where I had eaten together with my two brothers each and every evening of my childhood.

My mother was smiling enraptured and Elías Traúm was eating

placidly. I was the only one who seemed to grasp the absurdity of the situation, and I saw both of them as future cadavers enjoying their last supper.

'Let's go out for a walk, Elías,' I said to him, 'if you've finished eating.'

'I've finished, lad,' Elías answered me, and took a sip of tea.

My mother would serve tea even when the temperature was off the thermometer, and the miracle was that her guest always accepted it as if it would infallibly be refreshingly cool. It was boiled, sweet tea and I had got into the habit of drinking it at the worst moments of my life. It calmed me down.

'Elías looked you up in the phone directory and first he called Aunt Beatriz,' said my mother, calling him by his first name. 'Beatriz told him she didn't know your new number but she could give him mine, because she thought you had split up. But anyway she didn't have the number of the house where you lived with that girl, because in fact you were never married.'

Aunt Beatriz was my father's sister: she had always harboured the suspicion that Esther and I had married legally and with great fanfare, and that we hadn't invited her either to the ceremony or to the party.

'Señor Traúm called and asked for you,' said my mother, regaining her composure. 'And you know…I don't give out your phone number. So I ask, who is speaking, where do you live, give me your number and I'll get him to call you back.'

My mother had only just reached this level of security, obeying my pleas and protests, after handing out my number to anyone who asked for it, including maniacs.

'Señor Traúm told me he's come from Israel and that he had already met you. So I asked him if he knew Shula. Which Shula? He asked. Shula Wasserman, I said to him, who lives in Jerusalem, the same as you. Shula Wasserman, he said to me,' my mother raised her voice and Traúm sat there smiling, 'how could I not know her! She lives quite close to my house. In Ramat Eshkol. And I started shouting, Shula, so you know Shula! Of course I know her, he shouted!'

I could imagine the two of them shouting, unjustifiably exalted.

'I've been friends with Shula all my life, I told him,' said my mother.

'Hardly, mother,' I said. 'She went to Israel when she was fifteen years old.'

'Isn't that a lifetime?' said my mother. 'Do you think life begins only at fifteen?'

'You're right.'

'And I tell Elías, could you take Shula a present from me? If you see her, I say. I see her, he replied, I see her. And here we are.'

'I see,' I said. 'And what present are you going to send her?'

'Can you believe it, I haven't bought it yet? You'll have to come back, Elías.'

'It will be a pleasure,' said Traúm.

'What if señor Traúm turned out to be a murderer or a thief?' I asked. 'What if you were opening your door to a thief? Even a decent man can turn into a thief if you invite him into your home like that,' I said, as if I was the mother.

'Impossible,' said my mother. 'He knows Shula, he lives in Israel.'

'He might have lied to you.'

'I'm not fifteen years old,' said my mother.

'When did you last take a walk around this area?' I asked him.

'Twenty-one years ago,' said Elías.

'Would you like to take a guided tour?'

'That's one of the reasons I came over,' he answered.

Chapter fourteen

Do you really know Shula Wasserman?' I asked him when we were outside.

'Really,' repeated Traúm.

'She's the local girl who made good,' I said. 'She went off with the best of the local lads, to Israel. Not even to a kibbutz: he got a well-paid job in Jerusalem. She's the envy of all her neighbours here: lucky with money, lucky in love.'

'She's divorced,' Elías told me.

'Divorced?' I shrieked like a shrill fishwife.

'When I met her she was divorced. But she's still living in Jerusalem.'

'My mother has photos of her when she was fifteen years old. A pretty girl.'

'And a pretty woman,' said Elías.

'Well well,' I said. 'What do you mean when you say you knew Shula?'

'In the way you are asking me about now.'

'But she must be a good sixty now,' I said, alarmed.

'What if she is?' said Elías coolly. 'But I knew her when she was forty. Just divorced and in her prime.'

'My mother hasn't spoken or written to her for more than twenty years,' I said. 'What about you, how old are you?'

'Fifty-two.'

'That means...' I said.

'Yes,' Elías interrupted me. 'I was the oldest of the three musketeers, and now I look even older. We always look older in comparison with our dead friends,' he added.

'When they started the review, when they were fifteen...' I said, 'you were...'

'I was the oldie of the group, I was twenty-three. But they were more intelligent than me. There were two prodigies—not three. My role was as coordinator. The truth is I couldn't detach myself from them—they fascinated me.'

'But that means you couldn't have done high school together.'

'Guidi started high school when he was twelve. He could have started when he was eleven. We went to the same school but no, we didn't coincide there. I'd already left a year before he arrived.'

If we didn't slow down a bit we'd get to Ecuador and the end of the last part of the district before we really wanted to. We were both fast walkers.

I took his arm and made a gesture as if asking him to slow down a bit. I wanted our chat to go on in time and for the space never to end. Destiny had brought us together despite my worst fears, and it made no sense not to hear his story.

We would die like two good Jews: murdered for no reason.

'How did Pesce know you were coming?' I asked.

'By e-mail,' Traúm told me, and in that melancholic space between his words and the streets, the term sent a little shock wave like a glimpse of the future. 'I don't know how he got my e-mail address, but he began to write to me. About four years ago now. Or rather, he started writing to me because he found my e-mail address. I don't know how. He must have been playing around with the electronic directories on the Internet, and found me that way.'

'Where did you know each other from?'

'He used to work for the paper *El mundo*, together with Benjamín.'

'But wasn't *El mundo* part of the PRT?'

'While Benjamín was a Montonero, you mean? They thought he was salvageable—he had been a Trotskysite. Although they were already fighting with the Fourth International...but...' he stopped and made a gesture of impatience. 'All this useless stuff our memory stores away!' he said. 'I should clear it all out and make space for the memories I need!'

'They are inseparable, though,' I told him. 'You can't separate your friends from the stupid things they did. No way.'

'No way,' repeated Traúm.

'What job did you do?' I asked.

'I didn't work,' he replied.

'What?' I insisted. 'How did you live?'

'I got by. Let's say I was an architect.'

'No, that won't do at all. Aren't you going to tell me how you got by?'

'Not for the moment, no.'

'When are you going to tell me?'

'If and when I need to.'

'Huh,' I said. 'Of course, it all fits. I don't know what shit this is. Who are you, anyway? God knows why Pesce sent me.'

'Pesce, poor thing, all he did was to say hallo via e-mail. Now and then he would ask how things were going, how Israel was treating me. To tell the truth I didn't want to start writing to him. E-mail's brilliant for that. You can't write a letter saying, 'Hi how are you, I'm fine,' 'Thanks for asking, I'm fine,' 'Everything's fine here, all the best.' But in an e-mail you can write that and it's acceptable.'

'Was Pesce a Montonero too?' I asked him.

Finally I was doing an interview with him.

'On the fringes. He didn't know what to do. He wanted someone to show him.'

'From first to last,' I said, 'he denied being the one you'd told you were coming to Argentina.'

'That doesn't surprise me,' said Traúm.

'Why's that?' I asked.

And I was sure he would come out with another puzzle.

'If you walk straight on down Agüero,' said Traúm, 'towards Corrientes, is there still a bar there?'

'I think so,' I said. 'They do pizza and pasta.'

'In those days it was still a bar that served beer,' said Traúm, and then without a moment's hesitation he asked: 'Why don't Jews do confession?'

'I haven't the foggiest idea,' I said.

'But there's nothing to stop us hearing other people's confessions, is there?'

'I don't know.'

'I don't think anybody would be against a Jew hearing a confession. Otherwise Freud wouldn't have been able to come up with what he came up with, would he?'

'I'm not sure psychoanalysts would like the comparison,' I said. 'A confessor listens passively and hands out punishment.'

'And I listened passively to Pesce's confession,' said Traúm. 'But I didn't punish him. He hadn't really done anything that deserved punishment.'

'I can't imagine Pesce making a confession,' I said.

'You're not going to be able to imagine it now, either,' said Traúm. 'I'm going to tell you, and it's all true. Pesce met me in that bar I mentioned before, on Agüero and Corrientes, when he finished work,' began Traúm.

'But I thought the offices for *El mundo* were in El Bajo?'

'On Calle Sarmiento, the Avenida de Mayo end,' said Traúm. 'But Pesce wanted to talk away from his job. Not as far as the district of Once, which he knew was our patch, the three musketeers. Why did Pesce confess to me?'

'Haven't a clue,' I said.

'He started off by joining the party. Guidi and I used to meet up with Benjamín after work. In the summer he would join us for a few beers, and gin in the winter. He wasn't even with us for that long. He was the *goy* in the group, the non-Jew. He played a very limited part and was on the outside of things, really. He was on the periphery in every way—in the Montoneros, in our group, and in life. He was part of the periphery of life.

'We only let him come with us when we went to collect Benjamín. Pesce had very good information, and I see that he still has. He wasn't an organic militant, like Benja or Guidi. At the time he was in contact with the leadership of other parties, as well as informers. They weren't sparing in the information they gave him. Everybody used him, he was a kind of postman, a useful gossip.

'Guidi and Benja used to listen to him like a source of information, using him to "characterise" reality. I found him amusing. One thing was clear to me—with his information he was paying for our company. He was as alone as a dog. Is he still alone?'

'Apparently so,' I said, 'like a dog.'

'But when we talked about women he never opened his mouth. When Guidi joined the Montoneros he started cutting down on the pornographic decibels. Thank God Benjamín kept the same levels. I think we had the fact that he didn't sleep with "comrades" to thank for that. As far as I was concerned I enjoyed telling them about it as much as I did doing it. But Pesce never uttered a word. It was a revealing silence.'

'Homosexual,' I said.

'Not necessarily,' Traúm went on. 'At the end of the winter of nineteen seventy-six, just over six months before they killed Guidi, he arranged to meet me in that same bar. It was already impossible for me to meet up with Guidi and Benja in a bar. Pesce could still go out to the bars—he was on the edge of things.

'He called my house and arranged to meet up. I was surprised, alarmed and afraid. I called Guidi and Benja every day, but maybe they'd been murdered an hour or a minute before, and Pesce was calling to give me the bad news. But no, it wasn't that.

'At first I didn't want to. We'd stopped seeing Pesce. The newspaper *El mundo* had gone under by then. What did he want from me? I wasn't in the Montoneros, or in the ERP, or anything else. But

I was still afraid of a trap, for my friends. After all, we were the three musketeers.

'I agreed. Nothing worse could happen. It was a butcher shop here. If he had to tell me that my friends had died, I wanted to go. If he had to tell me they were about to be killed or caught, I wanted to go. And I had one real hope, that Pesce could give me a piece of information that would convince Guidi and Benja that they should leave the country. That Pesce would give me a photocopy of a decree ordering Benja and Guidi to be gunned down, and when I showed it to them it would be like a magic talisman that would guarantee their flight from the country. But it wasn't that. The decree was written and signed, but there was no photocopy.

'I told him I'd be there. And I went. Corrientes and Agüero. The Impartial bar. Pesce didn't beat about the bush.

'"They're going to kill us all," he said.

'"I'm already getting out of here," I said. "And they won't kill you."

'"Does it make any sense to you to go on living without your friend?" he asked.

'"They forgot that life makes any sense," I said. "Not me."

'But I didn't answer his question.

'"I have to tell you," said Pesce. "I'm not actually afraid of them killing me. I'm afraid they will kill the three of you and there will be nobody left to tell. You three are my only friends. I mean, the only people I talk to. I'm alone as a dog. At least with all of you I would get out to the bar."

'"Why me?" I asked. "Why don't you tell Guidi or Benja?"

'"They can't meet up in a bar," he answered.

'But I sensed another answer:

Because you are going to survive. I want somebody alive to know my secret. I'm alone too much. I don't want my secret to die with people who are going to die.

'"I like boys," said Pesce.

'For a split second I thought he was referring to Guidi and Benja, and this would be another explanation why he was meeting up with me and not with them. But it was just a split second, and then

I understood. Anyway, Pesce wanted to be absolutely clear. Looking at me without any expression in his eyes, he added:

'"Little boys."

'And again, more strongly this time:

'"Baby boys and girls."'

'What a bastard,' I said.

'No,' answered Traúm. 'He wasn't a bastard.'

'What do you mean, no?' I said. 'That really is off limits. Go to bed with whoever you want, they can be sixty or a hundred. But kids are sacred. That's the lowest of the low.'

'Kids are sacred,' Traúm acknowledged. 'And Pesce never touched them. He swore to me on everything he held sacred. He'd never touched them, never gone anywhere near them. He'd thought about getting married.'

My first thought was *Poor guy*, but I didn't say it.

'He had just one moment of weakness: he described to me the part of boys' bodies that he liked. How now and again, without meaning to, he would look at them. This was the only time, when he was describing this, that he couldn't conceal his lust. Afterwards, it was a confession. Solemn, controlled, tortuous. He didn't want us to be killed without knowing his secret. He was a bastard for other reasons,' said Traúm. 'He didn't give a fuck whether we were killed or not. We were the only people who'd made room at the table for him and he didn't give a fuck. He wanted to tell us his secret.'

'But you survived,' I said.

'He knew that,' said Traúm thoughtfully.

'Why did he send you those e-mails?'

'How the fuck do I know, man?' said Traúm distractedly. 'Maybe I really am the only person he ever told, and by exchanging the odd word with me he feels as if he really is talking to someone— maybe he feels less alone. Maybe I'm the only mirror he has. Maybe he told someone else and they got killed.'

'Do you think he could still swear today that he never touched a child?' I asked.

'I think so,' said Traúm.

'I wouldn't be surprised,' I said, 'if he hadn't regretted giving me this piece to do, that he was afraid his secret might come out and so he was behind everything that happened. Who else knew you were arriving?'

'No, it wasn't him,' said Traúm, sounding sure. 'He's not a man of passion. He was cursed with a terrible desire, but he was also blessed with an extraordinary capacity for repression. He told me that time: "I look at your friends, all those lads, saying they are looking for a better world, that they want a better world. Now they don't even say it, they're hiding away like crabs. But my question is, what better world could I live in? What the shit would socialism ever do for me? Do you know what my better world is? A world where it is isn't forbidden to fuck children, or a world where kids don't exist. What the fuck does the economy matter to me?"

'No, it wasn't him,' Traúm went on. 'I think I know who it is I'm irritating. And it's not that serious. Something to do with women,' he said.

'If I were you I'd get out of here tomorrow morning just the same,' I said.

'I can't,' he said. 'The last time I was in this country I had to leave without saying *kaddish* for my friends. I couldn't say a funeral prayer for them. They need one in order to reach heaven. What am I if not an old Jew? I have to meet their families, and ask them to take me to the cemetery so I can say *kaddish*.'

'I don't know if they'll be in the cemetery,' I said. 'I don't know if…if their bodies are there even.'

'I'll say *kaddish* in their houses,' said Traúm.

I was silent, and felt uneasy. I wanted him to leave the next day. I didn't want to have to say *kaddish* for anybody, I didn't even know how to say *kaddish*. My anxiety for his safety was more acute than my desire to know the truth that was beginning to come out.

'Let's go to the Impartial,' said Traúm. And he added in a dreamy voice: 'pizza and pasta.'

Chapter fifteen

Tucumán and Agüero was my favourite bit of town—in the Once district the sun rises and sets on this corner, the first star of the Sabbath appears on this corner, and on this corner you can choose the direction of your day. But on the short walk up to Agüero and Corrientes it came over me again that we were exposing ourselves to danger, both of us walking along quite openly beneath the gaze of our tormenters.

When we reached the bar I couldn't stop staring obsessively out of the window.

'They won't kill us in the open air, man,' said Traúm.

'That's what Benjamín thought,' I reminded him.

'They're not going to kill us at all,' stated Traúm. 'I told you, it's fine. They can kill us for any reason. But they won't kill us for this, that's for sure. Calm down. I know they were following me.'

'You knew they were following you? Did Pesce tell you?'

'No, I worked it out for myself. I know something about these things.'

'Where did you learn?'

'I was the friend of a number of lads persecuted in difficult times.'

'I imagine that for you the term "persecuted" doesn't imply greater moral or political value, is that right?'

'No, it doesn't,' acknowledged Traúm. 'Besides, I have more reason than you to hate the Montoneros organisation; I think that without it my friends would still be alive. Or an even more naïve thought: that without this organisation my friends wouldn't have thrown themselves over the edge. Both ideas are false. But what about you? Why does it repel you so much? Why do you despise them the way you do?'

'In the first place, that's the way it is,' I said. 'I don't like them. I don't like Firmenich, or his speeches, or his little ditties. But if you want me to spell it out…there is a photo where Firmenich and Galimberti are embracing Arafat, some time towards the end of the seventies, it must be. It was the time when the PLO was attacking children's kindergartens.'

'Maalot,' said Traúm.

'I don't speak Hebrew,' I told him.

'No need to,' said Traúm. 'Maalot was the city with the kindergarten that the PLO attacked. They killed sixteen children.'

'With a bomb?'

'No, bullets.'

'Isn't that enough to make you despise the Montoneros? But there's something even more important for me. After that embrace, how could a Jew belong to the Montoneros organisation?'

Traúm shrugged and looked out of the window. But without fear, just to look somewhere.

'Are you going to do this interview?'

'It depends on you,' I said. 'If you want to. I suppose there's no way you would leave Argentina right now?'

'No,' he answered. 'But I'll agree to the interview. Afterwards we'll see if it is publishable. That all right with you?'

'No problem,' I said. 'Besides, that gives me the chance to ask you things that are unpublishable.'

'Let's do it,' said Traúm.

'You are tossing me a number of enigmas,' I began, 'that you will have to clarify at some point. What I mean is, you're telling me half-truths because, I don't know why, you want to keep me guessing. Why did you tell me you didn't work, but you don't want to tell me how you got by? Why didn't you tell me straight away you were an architect? And what do you mean, when you say it's got something to do with women?'

'All right, all right,' said Traúm. 'I'll answer both questions at the same time. When I left the country, I left my whole past in darkness. My own past and the past of others. I was particularly careful that nobody should have information about what my life had been in Argentina, and I was just as careful to leave the lives of Guidi and Benjamín concealed. I wrote nothing, I said nothing, I didn't make the slightest effort to keep their memories alive. But now—this is the last time I'll set foot in Argentina.'

'How can you be so sure?' I interrupted him.

'I'm one hundred percent sure,' he said. 'The last time. That's why I'm hesitating to leave, why I won't listen to your advice. But I'm going through the same syndrome as Pesce: I want someone to know my secrets. Otherwise, I wouldn't have let him know I was coming. I wouldn't have walked back into a wasps' nest like this. But I left without anybody knowing—I wanted somebody to know I was coming back.'

He gazed around the bar, as if he was looking for friends or people he knew, or as if he just had to look around him for a few seconds for somebody to recognise him.

'I can't bring myself to tell you everything all at once,' he went on. 'And maybe we'll stop meeting and I won't have got over my fear, or the silence that kept me safe all those years. But I have one, faint hope, that when my plane takes off you'll know almost everything.'

'And what then?' I asked, alarmed.

'Then I'm going to change my name and address, and you'll never see me in your life again.'

'Can you do that?' I asked.

'I can,' he said in an assured tone. 'I know how to do it. And maybe I ought to do it.'

'Is this just the Pesce syndrome, is it just that you can't bear to be alone with your secret?'

'No. It's also part of the *kaddish*. There were three of us, and each of us had his own story. Are you going to show a bit of patience, or do I have to tell you what I meant when I said it was something to do with women?'

'I'll be patient,' I said, against my will.

I glanced out of the window. They could shoot at us from a car, or come in the bar and kidnap us. Traúm had brought his past with him. A portable past.

Chapter sixteen

Why did you call yourselves the "tres mosqueteiros" instead of the "tres mosqueteros"? Why did you add that extra "i" in the "musketeers"? It's like Portuguese,' I said, trying to bring some chronological and thematic coherence to this pretence of an interview.

'It's like Portuguese,' he acknowledged. 'But that's how don Pasquale, the local shopkeeper, deformed words, to make them sound Jewish. We were the three musketeers, no doubt about that. They were the two brilliant boys. I was the young idiot. They were prodigies, the pair of them, but they needed me. They needed my calm, a certain guidance, someone who could keep things peaceful as their talents developed. It's not often in Argentina you can find two boys of fifteen who have read, for themselves, the Torah, the Mishna, and the Talmud in the original. And who are secular. No, there's nothing common about that. When they were sixteen I would follow them around like a faithful dog. I was addicted to the taste of their knowledge. But they couldn't live. They couldn't live. I could live. We always went around the area together, I acted as timekeeper for them. We went from Guidi's house to a conference in la Amia. From Benjamín's house to a class in Hebrew Studies.'

'Did you never go elsewhere, to Israel?'

'Never,' said Traúm. 'At seventeen, Guidi wrote a pamphlet against Zionism. That caused a stir. He published it in his review, *God is silent*. No—any chance of getting invited to Israel was soon nipped in the bud. And who would invite us to Europe other than Jewish organisations?'

'What did you think of the article?'

'Terrible, a kowtowing to the worst Marxism, flying in the face of his own intelligence. I responded to it.'

'Ah,' I let slip. 'It was you. What were your surnames?'

'Guidi Mitzkeien.'

'Was his name Guidi, not Guido?'

'Guidi, Guidi Mitzkeien. Benjamín Janín. And you know my surname.'

'You were the three Russians,' I said.

'No; Guidi's grandparents came from Lithuania, and Benja's were from Poland.'

'What I meant was that none of you were Sephardic Jews.'

'No,' said Traúm. 'A bit of Sephardi might have done them good. Less cold, less vodka. More rhythm and sweets, a different climate. Maybe they would have borne their knowledge more serenely.'

'Well, tell me then. What were they like?'

'Can I finish telling you about the extra "i" in the "mosqueteiros"?'

'Please do.'

'The shopkeeper, don Pasquale, I don't know how old he was. A thousand. I think he'd seen the whole district become more and more Jewish. When he set up his shop, there must still have been Indians there. He was the only *goy* left by now. He called us all Jacoibs. "You Jacoibs," he used to say, "you take good care of your moiney like I take care of my doig."'

'Was he anti-Semitic?' I asked, laughing.

'As much as he needed to be. A picturesque, local anti-Semitism. "Why do you lot wear skull-caps?" But we still bought from his shop. We bought ham from him. He had a speech defect, and put an extra "i" into everything. "They're Jacoibs, but their moiney's still moiney."

"That Solomon, all skullcap and beard, but what goirgeous tits that Rebecca's goit that he's married." Yes, he sounded Portuguese, the idiot. For some reason or other we all called ourselves the "mosqueteiros" with the extra letter. We did, and so did other people too. It marked us out, defined us. We were the three Jewish "mosqueteiros". The extra "i" allowed us the epic without the assimilation.'

'Was it all conferences and debates? What about fun, what about girls?'

'Fun was one thing, girls were quite another, or rather, "the" girl. Which stopped being a game very early on. But we used to have fun on the *goy* corner.'

'What?' I asked.

'The *goy* corner. It was more than a corner. It was a tiny square, on Ecuador and Mansilla. A pathetic little square of concrete, earth and a couple of straggly trees. Not in Once, but in the Barrio Norte district. My home was in the Barrio Norte, but I felt I belonged in the Once. There we would play at not being Jews.'

'What?' I said again.

'We would play…' he said, and his voice broke, 'We would play…'

He had started to weep.

'No death frees you of the judgement of others,' he said, drying his eyes with a tiny napkin that dried nothing at all. 'But I played along with them. I played along with them. You can't expect me not to feel something for them.'

'It would never occur to me to expect anything like that,' I said, moved.

'I loved them. We would play. On the goy corner we would play at not being Jews. Our names were Pérez, González and López.'

'And what did you do?'

'We tried to behave as we thought non-Jews behaved. Sometimes we told anti-Jewish jokes. We would talk about circumcision as if we were not circumcised ourselves. We would feel sorry for the poor fellows who had to have this dreadful thing done to them. We would grab ourselves between the legs and give out fake moans of pain. We talked about cars and horses.'

'I know Jews who lose everything on the horses and pass the time talking about cars,' I said.

'For some of us, being a Jew is something else,' Traúm answered. 'And for each Jew, being a non-Jew is something different. That's how it was for us. Being a *goy* is a single and clearly defined category, just as being a Jew is for many *goyim*. We used to say we would get married to someone called Moria Casán, and that we would call our children Antonio, Jesús and Maria. We congratulated ourselves on being the religious majority in the country. We were *goyim*. On this corner.'

'What about when you left the corner?'

'We were really happy. I'd have to admit to you that it's a tense, edgy form of entertainment, but we played it.'

'The *goy* corner,' I said.

'The *goy* corner,' he repeated. 'Is it still Rabbi Rutman in the synagogue on Tucumán and Uriburu?'

'I don't know many rabbis,' I said. 'One or two, by sight. I don't know what synagogues they are in. I don't go to the synagogues.'

'Neither do I,' said Traúm. 'But I thought you might know this one, as it's just a block away from where your mother lives…'

I was alarmed to note that Traúm's memory had filed away information about the precise locality of my mother's house.

'What's the matter with you?' he asked.

'Nothing particular,' I said. 'Why?'

'Apart from this,' said Traúm. 'I can understand why you look out of the window every other second. But there's something else bothering you. I can tell you're on edge. Are you sleeping well?'

'I didn't sleep last night,' I said.

'Well, apart from being afraid, what is it?'

'Something to do with women,' I said.

'Are you ill?' he asked.

I stopped looking out of the window and ordered a milkshake of peach and milk, with lots of ice. Traúm was delighted; in Israel there was nothing like these enormous milkshakes in plastic cups that you found in the bars of Argentina.

'I've just split up,' I said. 'My wife asked me to leave.'

Traúm waved his arms as if inviting me to go on.

'I made a mistake,' I said.

The old liquidiser altered for one noisy moment the suffocating atmosphere in the bar, without improving it in the slightest.

'They're still using the same machines,' said Traúm. 'A mistake. Did you sleep with someone else?'

'I didn't even sleep with her,' I said. 'But yes, someone else.'

'Younger?' he asked. 'Prettier?'

'Much older, and a complete dog—a neighbour.'

'A neighbour? Are you totally stupid? I only recommend being unfaithful when you are travelling. For those hot-blooded things who have to do it in the same city, the girl should be at least three districts away. You should have to take at least two buses if you are going to ruin your life.'

'Are you married?' I asked.

'I was in a steady relationship, in Israel,' he said. 'But I never got married. Now we might say that I'm separated and happy.'

'Was she from Argentina?' I asked.

'No, she was Israeli,' he replied. 'Couldn't your wife forgive you?'

'It's not that she feels hurt,' I said. 'She feels uncomfortable. She doesn't need to forgive me. Obviously what I did didn't hurt her pride. After all, I deceived her with some sort of monster. There's no comparison between them. What's happening is that when I lie down next to her she sees the other woman. We're in the same building. When she sees me she sees her too. Esther finds it really irritating.'

'Esther? Like the queen in the Bible.'

'Yes. And I went out for a long time with a woman called Deborah. But that's it. Nobody's going to give me another chance. I'll have to look elsewhere for women.'

'If it's just that she's irritated,' said Traúm, 'she'll get over it. How did she find out?'

'I told her,' I said, as the milkshake arrived.

'Oh, you really are a fool twice over,' said Traúm, pouring himself a generous helping into a glass, the same amount again dripping down the side of the jug. 'They're still using the same jugs.'

'You have to be sure of what you're doing,' I said, making a very slightly better job of it. But still most of the liquid formed a little pool on the tablecloth. 'Children?' I asked.

Traúm took the glass away from his mouth.

'No, no children.'

I raised my glass to my mouth. I wanted to give him a moment to add something.

And indeed, Traúm said:

'There's not really any connection,' he said. 'But I had to look after the boys.'

He paused again. He took a sip of the milkshake, as if he was drinking coffee.

'I had to look after Guidi and Benjamín. I wasn't too good at it. I'm not cut out for looking after children,' he said.

'They were adults,' I said.

'Once I had a dream. I wasn't in Jerusalem. I'd gone to Beer-sheva, to visit someone or for work, it doesn't matter. But I stayed in a very nice hotel, and during a siesta one afternoon when it was very hot, I dreamed that Guidi and Benjamín were coming to Israel. I was going to meet them at the airport. But when they arrived, they couldn't get through the border controls that separate passengers from the people meeting them. I was alone in the hotel, nobody else took a siesta.'

'It's impossible to take care of a healthy adult,' I told him. 'I've often thought that. Everyone does just what he wants.'

'For a long time,' said Traúm, 'my job was to look after healthy adults. But you're right—everyone does exactly what they want. You can only take care of them if they don't notice. I'm going to see if I can find Rabbi Rutman. You never know, he might know something about the boys' families.'

He still called them 'boys'. But in 1977 Guidi was twenty-three and Benjamín was almost the same age.

'How old was the rabbi when you left?'

'Seventy or more,' said Traúm. 'But who knows, he might still be alive.'

'What did he think of the three musketeers?'

'That our intelligence was our curse,' said Traúm. And with the gesture typical of the people of Buenos Aires, he called the boy for the bill.

Chapter seventeen

Traúm wanted to go off to look for the rabbi and to wander around the district of Once on his own. Twice I offered to go with him, but he said no. We agreed to meet in Paraguay square at six o'clock the next evening. He wasn't sure yet how much longer he would stay in Argentina, but he promised me it wouldn't be more than two weeks.

I walked along Agüero towards Córdoba and found that I had nothing to do. Worse than that, since my chat with Traúm, the rest of my life seemed bland and colourless.

For a while this stretch of Calle Agüero had been a sort of mafia patch, moved in on by down-and-outs and drunks. The new shopping centre had civilised the area. Why had I told Esther about my miserable adventure? Why had I behaved like a bloody fool?

We were lying naked on the bed. Esther had rubbed aromatic oils into my skin and was telling me stories as she caressed me. She spoke of other men and other women. In one tale she stripped a friend of hers, slowly, down to her bare skin. In another story she summoned up a man: for my sake these had to be strangers. In another story she got me onto a bus and started to rub me against an enormous-arsed woman who was holding her adolescent daughter by the hand. I wanted this story to go on forever. I had rarely had such a good time in my entire life. And so I told her, as if it was just another story, what had happened with Delia. I called her Delia, I called him Darío, and I placed the whole thing on the tenth floor.

As we were getting dressed, Esther asked me with a half smile:

'That thing about Delia…is that true?'

And I was slow off the mark to answer. If I'd answered quickly I might have got away with it. If I'd said: 'Yes, it's true,' immediately, then there would have been a bewildered silence on her part, and then I could have said: 'No, darling. How could it be true?'

Or else I might just have said straight away, looking aston-ished:

'No, darling. How could it be true?'

But I'd hesitated. I'd looked at her with an expression that asked: 'Would you mind if it was true? Would you mind if I had this adventure so I could tell you about it later?'

That moment's delay in answering precipitated the catastro-phe. In the end, I didn't answer at all. There was no need. Esther had zipped up her skirt without asking for my help, and was marching quickly into the sitting room.

Chapter eighteen

And so it was that at five o'clock in the afternoon I had nothing to do. The sun was hanging motionless in the sky just as it did when God permitted Joshua to win his battle, but this time the sun was shining down not on my success but on my utter failure. The sky and the air were unmoving. People walked up and down the street, but the world was immobile and yellow. I had nothing to do and no desire to do anything, and I had decided not to go to the newspaper.

'I'll buy a bottle of whisky,' I thought to myself. 'I'll shut myself up in my room, in the dark, and I won't stop until I pass out. Tomorrow is another day.'

I bought a 75-cl bottle of imported whisky in a shop, given to me in a brown paper bag, and I hopped on a bus and got off two blocks from my house. I crossed to the shady side of the street, and as I walked along I gathered together some of the crumbs of my life: I could almost savour the moment in which I would drop onto my bed with the bottle of whisky by my side like a submissive slave.

I opened the door and heard noises. They were coming from my bedroom.

In my moment of panic an angel of the Lord stopped me from dropping the whisky to the floor where it would shatter into a thousand pieces. Olga appeared in the doorway, saying hallo or mumbling something.

It was cleaning day. The day after Esther and I split up my mother had found a woman to come and clean my flat. She discussed it with Esther first, of course. My mother and Esther were still right beside me. Although my mother didn't know why we had separated she had no doubt it was my fault. And she was right.

I asked Olga if my room was done, and she said it was as she headed towards the kitchen.

When we passed each other—I was headed straight for my room clutching my bottle—her elephantine buttocks were just centimetres away from me. I made space for her to pass, but when I fell onto my bed I found I had a notable erection.

'After all,' I said to myself as I unscrewed the red plastic cap, 'I'm alone in my house with a woman. It's normal to feel a certain level of excitement.'

Olga was obscenely obese for her small frame. She had a definite hook to her nose, but the rest of her face was lost in an amorphous mass. Yet, you could just make out some features which revealed someone who was still only a girl.

She was somewhere between twenty-five and thirty years old.

I'd never done it with a cleaning woman.

I'm talking about life in general.

At least forty percent of men who were in the same year as me at school had been granted the favours of a cleaning woman, either their own or in somebody else's house.

I took a second large slug of whisky and wondered why not. All throughout senior school I'd kept away from prostitutes or domestic cleaners: I'd condemned myself to starting off when I was eighteen, in a loving conquest. Why didn't I make up a bit for lost time, seeing that my search for love had proved fruitless?

'No,' I answered my own question. First of all, because most likely Olga would give me a wallop with one of her short but hefty arms. And in the second place because her girth is not normal, but suggests a glandular problem. Olga isn't physically normal. Maybe at the crucial moment she would start to dribble. Or maybe her naked body would hold surprises for me that, frankly, I would rather not uncover. And what if I go ahead and she goes and tells my mother? The whole of Once would know I had gone completely mad. My mother would draw the shop curtains and tear her clothes.

I opened the door a few centimetres, poured myself another little bit of whisky and sat down heavily on the floor. Olga was carefully scrubbing away at the kitchen sink, and her buttocks swung from side to side like an overloaded ship in the middle of a storm. I began to rub myself too.

I'd forgotten to stop tilting the bottle of whisky as I pulled it away from my mouth and a few drops of liquid fell onto my neck. I came to a little and stood up. If I didn't get out of the house as fast as possible I would be heading straight into the kitchen and placing myself right behind Olga. After a few moments of pretend refusal—like the story of the fat woman on the bus—Olga would let me lift up her skirt and satisfy myself right there. She would dribble and then she would ask me for money. For once, I had to say no. I had to choose life.

I stumbled out of my room, mumbled good-bye to Olga and I was already in the elevator by the time I got my trousers properly back on.

I took a taxi and gave him the newspaper address.

I arrived there at seven in the evening. I saw the time on the taxi clock.

'Do you work here?' said the taxi driver admiringly.

'Of course,' I answered.

In reception Fabiana was chatting comfortably with a couple of guys who looked like bouncers. The two of them were in suit and tie, and had obviously left their dark glasses somewhere. They seemed to be waiting for someone, but meanwhile were quite happy to while away the time by flirting with the receptionist.

There was not a single trace of the hard-faced Fabiana who usually greeted me with a fixed grimace on her puckered lips. She was chatting away with them, the slut, the whore. Her breasts, which were normally concealed as jealously as the rest of her body behind the counter, were now generously exposed to the eyes of the two bouncers. They were abundant, yet vulgar; snugly between them hung a little chain with a golden 'F' on the end of it. Just as I was resigning myself to the fact that I had no part to play in this amiable interchange and was walking over to my desk, Fabiana stood up, and without giving me the time to silently thank my good fortune, she shifted her body from behind the counter, offering for the first and perhaps last time the chance to weigh up the value of her inaccessible rear end.

One of the bouncers stood in front of me, and leaning on the reception counter as if he was a regular in a disco waiting to be served, he prevented me with his well-endowed thoracic cage from following the equine and despair-inducing gait of Fabiana as she made for the secret entrance that led to the offices of the senior management of the paper.

I continued on my way—the common entrance of employers with lowly responsibilities—and at my desk I found, typing hard, my friend and colleague Guillermo Pablani. We occupied similar positions on the paper, me and Pablani. We both possessed a vocation for uselessness, the difficulty of being boxed into a particular corner and the intelligent submissiveness of those who know that any task assigned to them is a sign of the good will of their employers. But I couldn't help observing that Pablani was sitting at my desk and using my keyboard. While his own desk and keyboard next to a pile of wires were occupied by a young electrician, a kind of dummy who was desperate to 'join in the fray' of journalism, and who at this moment was to be seen head down in an attitude of exaggerated concentration, with the enthusiasm of a hamster running on a new wheel.

'Pesce told me to sit here,' Pablani said somewhat uneasily. 'How do you open Word? I'm writing with a really crap programme here, no s's, no accents, nothing.'

I didn't answer him—an involuntary discourtesy brought on no doubt by the alcohol I had consumed—and changed direction as if rolling down a hill towards Pesce's office.

Señor Pesce was busy. But he was polite enough to take advantage of his glass office to wave to me to wait.

Opposite him a well-endowed woman was showing off her not unappreciable thighs. Her dark hair was perfectly groomed. An elegant little green suit with a brooch, and she only had to sit there for you to want to see her in every conceivable position. I knew her from somewhere. If only the whisky fumes would clear for a moment, I could set to one side of my imagination the photographs of a naked body in movement and use the rest of my memory to try and remember where I knew her from. But neither the whisky fumes nor my memory were in any hurry to come to my assistance: I imagined her sitting over me, behind me, me lying down and her sitting up, groaning against a mirror, rising and falling, leaving a misty patch on the mirror exactly the same size as her now small, now gigantic, mouth.

Pesce made a reverential gesture towards the woman and she stood up. She left the office and passed by me without seeing me, leaving behind her a waft of her indefinable essence like someone tossing a coin to a beggar. I know that people in Buenos Aires call women with exuberant breasts and hips goddesses, but not me. This one, however, was a goddess. I remembered who she was. In the days when I used to read the papers she was in them almost every day. She was Secretary for Health and Social Action. One of those women who never stop being forty-three years old. Cristina Sobremonte.

Strangely enough she only had one surname. When she appeared in my memory I felt that I was missing a surname. But she only had the one. It was a shame: I wanted to roll around with her in the garden of her mansion with her two surnames firmly fixed.

Pesce told me to come in and sit down. Trying to avoid any further errors, I asked him:

'Any chance of a coffee?'

'No,' said Pesce. 'I've got some good news for you.'

The glass of Pesce's office still held the damp smell of perfect animal, the smell of señora Sobremonte. But what would Pesce care about that? He could only be interested in the basic perfume of infant schools. Cristina would have to lose more than thirty-three years off her age, at least, before she could be of the slightest interest to him.

Would Pesce know I knew his secret? His protruding upper lip offered no response.

'I'm going to give you some leave, Mossen,' he continued. 'Two weeks. On full pay, of course.'

'Am I in danger, señor Pesce?' I asked, alarmed.

'Not for a moment,' replied Pesce in a reassuring tone of voice. 'As far as I am concerned your safety is absolutely guaranteed. But you must understand that I can't stop you putting yourself in danger. I can throw you a life belt—but don't ask me to empty the oceans!'

'You can't look after healthy adults,' I said.

'Your safety is guaranteed, your job is secure. What about your sobriety, is that guaranteed?'

Clearly his inability to perceive the aroma casually abandoned by Cristina didn't prevent his sense of smell picking up my breath.

'Of course,' I said. 'I'm a feature writer. I don't want to make trouble for anybody.'

'What about a little trip?' he asked.

'A piece for the paper?' I asked in my turn.

'No,' he said. 'Mar del Plata, Miramar…take those two weeks' holiday.'

'I'm not a sun-worshipper,' I said. 'I don't like it. Although who knows…'

'I'll call you in two weeks' time,' he said to me. 'If I don't call you, don't worry—it just means your leave is automatically extended. I'm guaranteeing your job. Don't worry about it. Wait for me to call.'

'All right,' I agreed, as the whisky-induced haziness finally started to recede. 'I suppose I can't ask any more questions.'

'Personnel have already been informed,' said Pesce, inviting me towards the door. 'Strangely enough you are one of the people most often on the premises and with the most holiday owing.'

I left his office with a servile nod of my head by way of saying good-bye. I threaded my way through the labyrinth of disks and hurried my step in order to not have to answer Pablani, who was already raising his head to ask me once more how to open Word.

I stood in the street outside for a moment to think about my next move. Night was slow in coming and on the opposite pavement the secretary, or undersecretary, I couldn't remember, of Health and

Social Action, one of the bouncers by her side, was waiting for the other one to open the door of the black saloon car with its official number plates. The slightest of breezes lifted her skirt by a few millimetres and I found myself staring at the front of her thighs. They were like fruit—mangoes, or peaches.

The car took her away, but the image of her thighs lingered in the hot air. I remembered a summer in La Falda, Córdoba, with my parents. My father was still alive then. I must have been nine or ten years old. My mother was talking to other women in the foyer of the hotel, women she just happened to meet. They were sitting in the armchairs in the reception area, in shorts or in long native skirts. I was sitting on the floor playing with a doll called Temerario, a plastic soldier. From where I was I could see the legs of a woman who was talking to my mother, sitting opposite her. I could see more than her legs. I could see the hidden part of her thighs that the skirt concealed. I could even see the beginning of darkness and the light colour of her underwear. I placed Temerario in a way that justified me lying down with my face against the carpet, without losing sight of the enemy position. Rita, as I called her as time went by, was crossing and uncrossing her legs. She would laugh, shift position and chat cheerfully. And then I caught a glance, a look, a sort of mute and gestureless wink, and I discovered she knew I was looking at her. She was doing it deliberately. She was doing it as a gift for me.

Chapter nineteen

The house, tidy and clean now, seemed fresher. The order in the house refreshed my brain, too. Women who cleaned other people's houses, and my house in particular, were, for me, endowed with a biblical resonance.

What was the good deed that lay behind the hospitality with which Sarah had welcomed in the three men sent by the Lord? Welcoming contemporary man into a tidy house.

We were all guests, sent by nobody in this incomprehensible world, and whoever welcomed us in with a made bed and clean kitchen deserved all the gratitude of which we were capable. I blessed Olga a number of times—it was a shame that her name had no biblical equivalent, nothing even close—and I thanked my lucky stars for my chaste decision that evening.

It was ten in the evening. I stretched myself out on my bed, and this time I would lie there until sleep came. I hadn't checked the answering machine.

I went back on my word to myself, and walked though to the sitting room, the third and final room of my miniscule apartment.

There were no messages. Why were there no messages? Why hadn't my mother phoned? Did my leave of absence include her as well?

Were we really protected? Was there any guarantee? Even though this was a time of night that she might begin to consider as being 'late', I called her.

She answered straight away in a singsong voice.

'Elías is washing the dishes,' she said.

'Elías who?' I asked.

'Elías, the Israeli,' she told me.

Anyone would think it was a description of one of the wrestlers in *Titans on the Ring*.

'He's not Israeli,' I said.

'Of course he is,' she told me, and I got the impression she checked with him, even though I heard nothing. 'He was born in Argentina, but he emigrated.'

'And what's he doing at your place?' I asked.

'He came over to pick up my present for Shula,' said my mother, surprised that I didn't know. 'I bought one for her. I couldn't let him go without having dinner. He's washing the dishes. Do you think your father ever washed the dishes?'

'Men shouldn't wash dishes,' I said in defence of my father. 'Tell him I'll meet him in the square tomorrow.'

'Yes, fine,' said my mother.

'Fine,' I said. 'Sleep well.'

'You too,' she said, and hung up.

'I suppose,' I said, to the silence coming from the phone, 'that he'll go and sleep in his hotel, won't he?'

I took *The War of the Jews* off my bookshelf and set myself to read a few chapters, which would take me to the point where I could appropriately phone the Juncal Hotel, just to make sure that old Elías really would be spending the night in the solitary bed in which he belonged.

I looked at the bottle of whisky, still standing on the floor, like a sentinel arrived just in time, after cutting, to fool his superior. Not a drop more, I said to myself.

I took the top off and drank the last toast to the evening.

Just as Eliezer was asking the zealots what was the point of a life without God, I fell asleep.

Chapter twenty

I t wasn't that bad: the bottle was still half full. It was eleven o'clock in the morning and the whisky did its country of origin proud—I had no hangover. I couldn't remember sleeping so well or so long for years.

'Esther and the rest of the world can go do what they want,' I said to myself. 'I'm young and healthy. A man of reasonable culture and with plenty before him. What do I care if Traúm stayed the night at my mother's house? It was time she had a boyfriend.

She's been more than faithful enough to my father's memory.'

A glass of orange juice, the morning paper and a pleasant chat with the barman. Life was waiting for me.

I went down to the bar on the corner—two blocks away, on Avenida Córdoba—and asked for orange juice, a double espresso, toast and the newspaper.

It was one of the better ones. It was better written, it carried more news, and as if that wasn't enough, I wasn't one of its journalists. Even better, it had a photo of Cristina Sobremonte, on page 15.

I don't know what effect it has on readers to come across the image in the paper of a person they saw in the flesh just a few hours before. But I began to bend my head down as if, in that photo, I could pry even further under her skirt. She was getting married.

The colour feature article announced that our lady was marrying a rancher who owned half the country, Ignacio Ruiz Reches.

Finally the cold logic of the universe was asserting itself, and Cristina would have not two but three surnames. I was happy for her, even though this put an end once and for all to my dreams of frolicking with her in the garden of her mansion.

No way, I thought. What would happen if I lay in wait for her and jumped on her in the fields belonging to Reches? They'd set the dogs on me, the farmhands would kill me or the bovine mass would trample me down, not out of malice perhaps but simply unaware of the danger of their specific weight.

The coffee put me in an even better mood. Cholo, the lad behind the bar—who I silently rebaptised Choco when he brought me my boiling or lukewarm coffee—told me that San Lorenzo had won the football. He was happy, and so was I.

I left the bar and went back home planning to continue my good mood in the bathroom. Such was my serene frame of mind that when the phone rang I let the machine pick up the message.

I heard Esther's voice. I turned on the shower thinking I would call her after washing. But I left the water running and went into the sitting room.

I dialled the number as I listened to the message:

'I was just calling to see if you were all right, after what you told me. Call me when you can. Kiss kiss.'

I was naked as I listened and called, and I placed this kiss where it suited me.

She answered.

'Are you all right?' I said anxiously. 'Is everything all right?'

'Sure,' she said. 'I just called to see if you were all right.'

'Great,' I said. 'I'm absolutely fine. Well, now that you've called me, not that great. This is the first morning I've managed to have breakfast without thinking about you all the time.'

'I'm sorry,' she said. 'I had to make sure you were all right. I was worried.'

'That's fine,' I said, 'that's fine. Are you in your dressing gown or are you already dressed?'

'In my dressing gown,' she said without thinking. 'I'm going in late today…'

She stopped. She realised what I was up to.

I immediately changed my infallible strategy to stop her hanging up on me.

'Are you off somewhere? Are you working out of the house today?'

Esther worked for a North American milk company, sending reports and accounts from its Argentine and Latin American subsidiaries. For a while she had spent three hours a day working in some office in the city centre, and our house was still awash with stamps from American Venezuela, Columbia, Guatemala and Chile. But since the arrival of the Internet her work had become almost entirely home-based. She also gave private lessons in Hebrew and English in the house we shared together. But I had never learned a word of Hebrew.

'There's an international conference for audiologists,' she told me. 'It's being held just out of town, and I've been asked to do simultaneous translation.'

'Good money?' I asked.

'Yes, fine.' She started to wind up the conversation. 'You're all right, then?'

'Absolutely,' I said.

We hung up.

I walked back to my room, trying to keep my mind blank. *The War of the Jews* was still lying on the carpet. Next to it was the bottle of whisky. The shower was still running like a telephone that nobody wants to answer.

Chapter twenty-one

Y ou're completely pissed!' Traúm said to me.
    He wasn't quite right. I was stumbling a bit, I was dodging
nonexistent obstacles, and I sat down on the bench in the square
with a mixture of relief and apathy, but there was still a quarter of a
bottle left when I emerged from my room.
    'I had a drop of whisky,' I said in a voice I barely recognised.
'That's all. Let's go and get a coffee.'
    I admit we had to wait while I vomited beside an unfortu-
nate old, leafy tree. Somebody had taken a key to its knotty trunk
and carved two initials inside a heart, but I didn't bother to try and
make them out.
    'Better?' asked Traúm.
    'Yes, I feel much better,' I said, trying to capture a mouthful
of air in that wall of heat.
    We looked for a bar along Marcelo T. de Alvear, passing
beyond Rodríguez Peña. Down this end Marcelo T. became a nice
road, shady and quiet.
    'I'll have a beer,' I asked Traúm.
    'Two coffees,' he asked the barman.

We were sitting at a table in the shade outside. I took advantage of the free glass of water to take a mouthful of water and spit, without anyone seeing me, into the gutter. Miraculously, the air moved beside us.

'Nice here, isn't it,' said Traúm.

'God be praised,' I replied thankfully. 'Are you planning to visit just Buenos Aires?' I asked, resigned to the fact that he would not be getting on his plane in the next five minutes.

'I'd like to take a short trip to Mar del Plata,' he said. 'And to Córdoba. I didn't find Rabbi Rutman, though. Nobody knew him. I want to pick up the trail, something familiar. Maybe I won't have enough time.'

Yes, if you waste it having dinner at my mother's... I thought to myself.

'Do you think the rabbi could have died?' I asked. 'Why don't you ask at the local council?'

'No, it's all right to flush the partridge out a bit, but not too much. They're not in the phone book. I mean, there are loads of people called Janín, but I don't want to start calling them all.'

'Why would you like to go to Córdoba then?' I asked. 'I was thinking about Córdoba today in fact, about La Falda.'

'That's amazing!' he said. 'Why?'

'You tell me first why you are yelling like that,' I replied.

'If I can, I'll go to La Falda,' said Traúm. 'I spent two summers there with Guidi and Benjamín. The first time, the lads were eighteen years old. They'd got out of military service, both of them. Guidi because of low numbers that year, Benja because his parents paid up.'

'What about you?' I asked.

'Flat-footed and shortsighted,' he said.

'You don't look shortsighted,' I said.

'I don't have flat feet either,' he answered. 'Do you want to hear?'

I nodded. My stomach was still in revolt and my pressure was going down. I had no idea what 'pressure' meant.

'Guidi had been invited to give a talk on mathematics and the Torah at a conference of mathematics going on in the Norto Marza hotel, which belongs to an Armenian guy.'

'I know that one,' I said.

And I added:

'My ex-wife is at a conference now, too.'

'He asked us to go with him. Benja helped him prepare his talk. It wasn't a Jewish conference or anything, just mathematicians. And they'd invited him. It was one of those conversations I had no hope of contributing to. I didn't understand a word. They just carried me along with them.'

'Why did you go then?'

'Travelling with them was always exciting. Besides, I don't know why, trips always seemed to me a great sexual offer: as a traveller you always manage to get something.'

I hope that excludes my mother, I thought.

'On that trip, Guidi was beginning to get over his lefty views a bit. Science was some help. Hard science is always a route back to life. Not back to earth necessarily, but back to life.'

'That's an original thought,' I said. 'A lot of mathematicians see it differently. My older brother is a mathematician, I think he sees it like you do.'

'As well as that,' Traúm went on, 'the two of them had only just got out of doing military service and the organic left, in those days at least, approved of obligatory military service. This was another thing that drove them away from Marxism. They were easier in their minds now.'

'I don't know if I've already asked you this,' I said. 'But if they were so intelligent and so erudite, how come they fell in with the Montoneros and organisations like that?'

'I don't know if I've already told you,' he mimicked me, 'but I don't have the foggiest idea. Like I said, Marxist thinking is a virus that gnaws away at your mind. It attracts you, then it swallows you up. As they would have it, it's a dialectical movement. Look at Althusser, he used to beat his wife. Do you want to hear about Córdoba or not?'

I promised to be quiet. This was a defect that spoilt my best interviews: I had the bad habit of talking more than the person I was interviewing.

'Guidi gave a talk that must have been brilliant, judging by the applause. I didn't understand a word. But we had a good time. I went to bed with a girl who worked at the hotel, a descendant of German immigrants with a local accent. Extraordinary. Benjamín got involved with the daughter of the people who owned the hotel opposite, because we were there for two weeks, one for the conference and the second on our own account. And Guidi...'

He took a sip of coffee and waited for another wisp of breeze, which never arrived. A muscle twitched in his throat as he swallowed.

'Guidi,' he continued, 'discovered a place in the mountains. It took something like an hour to get up there. It was wonderful. There was a stream running down and the air was fantastic...like my mother used to say, it smelled like eucalyptus. We went up there. Guidi had come across a kind of natural corral, up on a plateau, with wild horses. A dozen or so horses racing around. That in itself would have been enough to make the pretty steep climb worth it. But there was something else. The corral was a stretch of land surrounded by rocks. If you went over these rocks there was another corral, another place that was very similar, also naturally formed. This second corral was empty, or nearly empty, with just two or three horses. And then Guidi said to the two of us, look, and we looked.

'We saw what he was looking at. It was a stallion mounting a donkey. An enormous-looking, majestic stallion. Mounting a poor female donkey who put up with him patiently. The other two or three horses seemed to be waiting in line.

"It's a mule factory," said Guidi, smiling. 'I don't know if they leave them together deliberately, or if it's mother nature.'

'We went back down after that, and I was feeling really horny. I had to wait until the German girl finished serving afternoon tea. Benjamín set off as fast as he could in search of his girl. Guidi sat in the hotel bar and started writing something or other. He never wrote literature.

'We went back the following year. Benja's girlfriend had got married in the meantime and was pregnant, even though she was so young. My girl found herself another job, in Villa Carlo Paz, the owner told me. We went up the mountain, of course, but the horses and the donkey had gone.'

'Can I get a Coca-Cola,' said Traúm to the barman.

'Pepsi all right?' replied the barman.

Traúm said yes.

'What about you?' he asked. 'What happened to you in Córdoba?'

'Something about a mule, too,' I said. 'I remembered today because I saw...it sounds half stupid.' I stopped.

The Pepsi arrived and Traúm invited me with a gesture to go on.

'But today I saw a woman's legs,' I said, settling into my now permitted role of narrator, 'and they reminded me...I saw the legs of a real woman,' I said, wanting to pay homage to Cristina Sobremonte before she turned into Mrs Reches, my farewell to the single woman. 'A woman. Cristina Sobremonte Reches. She's our Secretary, or underSecretary, of Health and Social Action.'

'She's getting married,' said Traúm.

'How do you know?' I asked him.

'I saw it in the paper,' he said. 'I read the paper in the hotel.'

'Well,' I said, 'those legs reminded me of a time in La Falda...'

'Anyway,' said Traúm, usurping my role of annoying interviewer who constantly interrupts the interviewee, 'I know her.'

Chapter twenty-two

I know her,' repeated Traúm, to my astonishment. 'Amazing whore.'

I raised my eyebrows questioningly: I wasn't sure if he was flattering her or insulting her.

'Thirty years ago,' said Traúm, 'if I'd heard anybody say anything about her I'd have thumped them in the mouth. But there's nothing I can do about it now.'

'Are you going to tell me where you know her from?' I asked with false brightness.

'She was our donkey,' said Traúm seriously. 'Our impossible love. I mean,' he went on, 'it was impossible for any of us, because she loved all of us. We weren't the type to suffer for love, but that was one thing, maybe the only thing, that we couldn't share. Anyhow, somehow, we shared it.'

'I can cope with ellipses and beating round the bush on any other subject,' I told him, 'but you have to spell this one out for me.'

'She was the one who sent the warning,' said Traúm promptly.

'Her?' I repeated disbelievingly.

'Or her future husband,' said Traúm. 'They don't want a bleeding hunk of the past for a wedding present.'

The words 'bleeding hunk,' while retaining their metaphoric quality, nonetheless acquired a considerable level of vulgarity.

'Unlikely,' I said. 'Do you really think Reches is going to be bothered by a relationship his future wife had with some Montoneros? You can tell you've been out of the country. People who used to kidnap businessmen are now working as bodyguards for them. And if you've been part of an armed movement, especially the Montoneros, it can give you a certain cachet, it's even quite chic in some social circles.'

'It's nothing to do with politics,' said Traúm. 'It's something ancestral.'

'Religious?' I asked.

'No!' shouted Traúm, amused at the idea. 'Religion? No! It's like this,' he lowered his voice and his tone. 'It's one thing for somebody to kidnap a businessman, and then that businessman discovers that the only way to sleep peacefully in his bed is to buy up the person who crops up in his nightmares. That's one thing. It's another matter altogether when your wife has been fucked in the arse by three of them together. When the whole world knows your wife was doing one of them while another was doing her and the third one was watching. That's a different thing altogether. These scenes don't fade with time, and the best you can hope for is that nobody else comes to hear about it.

'Are there any photos?' I asked lasciviously.

'No, of course not,' said Traúm, offended. 'We were young, passionate, but not perverted. We loved her.'

'And what about her, what happened to her?'

'She,' said Traúm, 'she was Jewish, did you know that?'

'*Marrana*? A Jewish convert to Christianity?'

'No,' Traúm said. 'just the opposite. She was the daughter of a Christian family, but she converted to Judaism.'

'And then she converted back again?' I asked, perplexed.

'What does conversion mean, anyway?' interrupted Traúm.

'They put you in a bathtub, say a few prayers over you in Aramaic or whatever it is. All superstitious nonsense. Conversion doesn't exist. But she was Jewish for a couple of years, then she stopped. These things happen. Anything can happen.'

Traúm's Pepsi was half empty and maybe it had got warm. He raised his hand and called the waiter over.

'Can I get a small Fernet?'

Even the mention of an alcoholic drink turned my stomach.

'And another Pepsi?' asked the waiter.

'No,' answered Traúm. 'I'll have it with the rest of this one.'

The waiter left to deal with the order and Traúm continued:

'She was a nice girl, high-class and physically splendid. Then suddenly she converted to Judaism, she became revolutionary and hid her wonderful tits under hippy clothes.'

His eyes relished the image of a memory projected in midair.

'I think she suffered a fit of normality. "Why am I doing this to myself?" she must have wondered. And she accepted all the gifts life gave her, being lovely, rich and beautiful.'

'I'll tell you straight,' I insisted for the umpteenth time. 'If you don't spell everything out and give me all the details, especially the sexual ones, I'm going to get very annoyed.'

'All right,' said Traúm. 'In that case I'll tell you in words of one syllable. As far as the exact order in which things happened is concerned, don't ask the impossible. I'll tell you but I might dot around a bit. But I don't mind if you ask questions.

'Cristina's mother was married to a man of good family. Not as rich as Reches, but he had plenty. The little I knew about the man was that he lived like a drunk. I mean, he was well-off, but he threw it down the drain. Cristina's mother loved him and put up with his drunkenness, despite all the trouble he got into. Because as well as a drunk he was a playboy and a swindler—by vocation, because he had enough money of his own. Cristina didn't talk about her biological father very much. She never seemed to have much affection for him, but she didn't hate him either: she remembered him with sadness. Cristina's mother, Miranda, started seeing a psychologist, she was so desperate about the hell her life had turned into. She couldn't leave him. This was nineteen sixty-four, nineteen sixty-five, and people were starting to go and see psychologists for things like that.

'During this same period the guy, Cristina's biological father, got some sort of illness, as a result of his alcoholism, that left him an invalid. A vegetable.

'He lost everything. Her in-laws started to put Miranda on a fixed income and her own family took the rest.

'She still went to see the psychologist. Torchinsky. Who from his B.A.Hons in Psychology soon became the sparkling new husband.'

The waiter brought the Fernet already poured into those strange little metal goblets, which Traúm turned upside down and poured into his glass. He drank it with relish.

'I never ordered Fernet in Israel,' said Traúm. 'I never even looked for it in the supermarket. I don't know if they have it over there. I've only just remembered it exists. It's so good.'

'I find it very bitter,' I said, 'but my father always used to drink it.'

'Señora Miranda Vellini of Sobremonte was transformed into Miranda Torchinsky. She stepped into the ritual Jewish bath, the *Mikve*, she recited the *shema* prayer, and the world welcomed a new Jew. She was happy to flee and take refuge amongst the people of Israel. And Dr Torchinsky, a B.A.Hons if you please, couldn't complain. I knew señora Miranda late on when she was fading and ill, but even then you could make out what must have been an arse worthy of consideration and a pair of shoulders that spoke of having sustained breasts not beneath mention.'

'Is there any woman you wouldn't have?' I asked.

He didn't reply. And I couldn't answer my own question. Immediately I wanted to ask him a question that might just stop him in his tracks:

'Did you sleep with my mother?'

No. It was still too soon to ask this dreadful question.

'They converted the girl, too,' said Traúm. 'I'm not really sure what conversion ceremonies are like, but I don't like them anyway. All that stuff about ritual bathing—like I said, it's just superstition.

Circumcision, on the other hand, seems more normal to me. I haven't the faintest idea what it's for or what it means, but it seems acceptable to me. But "conversion", what is that? Belonging to a people can't be just like changing a television channel. I'm not a gatekeeper for any temple: if anybody wants to come in, let him in. If you want to be a Jew, you are a Jew. Now, if you are born a Jew, I'm sorry, but you can't be anything else. The entrance is free, but for those who are born Jewish there is no way out. So, you want to be a Jew? Fine, be a Jew. But without all this fuss, without being a "convert". What does it mean to be Jewish, anyway?'

'Oh please,' I said, 'let's not start…'

'No,' laughed Traúm. 'It's a joke. Let's go on. So, all of them were Jews: the university B.A.Hons Torchinsky, Miranda and Cristina. For the ex-señora de Sobremonte it was a cataclysm, going from waiting for her husband to get back from wherever he'd been to waiting for the doctor—sorry, B.A.Hons!—Torchinsky to stop being so attentive. Listening over dinner to book commentaries and elegies of Che Guevara, and other commentaries on the "experience" of Velasco Alvarado. Do you know who Velasco Alvarado was?'

'Yes,' I said. 'A dictator.'

'In those days he was called a "soldier of the left". Did I already tell you what I thought of the thinking of the left? But let's not get sidetracked again. I imagine señora Miranda must also have enjoyed the first gentle caresses of her life, it must have been the first time a man bothered to try and please her. A man who made an effort to find her "erogenous zones" while he spoke to her of the latest developments in teaching policy for the oppressed peoples of Latin America. I don't know how much Miranda must have appreciated this shift in sexual politics: maybe she preferred señor Sobremonte arriving home drunk, tearing off her nightdress and spreading her arse against the kitchen table, without waiting for her to wake up properly. I don't know.'

'Your sexual fantasies are so similar to mine it's scary,' I ventured.

'Are there any other kind?' asked Traúm.

'I don't know if Miranda was happy,' Traúm went on. 'Happiness is one thing and being at peace another. Sometimes we have to give up on happiness in order to be able to go on living. You see?' Traúm stopped for a moment. 'That's what being a Jew is for me— knowing that life is more important than happiness.'

Chapter twenty-three

When Cristina appeared among us,' Traúm went on, 'when we "saw" her, she was sixteen years old. She was a Jew and she was on the left. I don't understand,' he continued, 'how it is that as time went by she became so much more beautiful. At the time I would have said there was nothing particularly memorable about her body. Guidi maintained—and I agree with him—that the ideal of feminine beauty doesn't change with time. Sofia Loren and Ava Gardner would have been considered lovely in any age. Gentle breasts and white teeth are already considered desirable in the *Song of Songs*. The idea that women exist whose loveliness is obvious goes back to the time of Abraham, whose wife was "pleasant to look at". Maybe there are some slight oscillations, obsessions at particular times with fat or skinny women, but that's nothing more than faddishness. For Guidi, Cristina could pass through the ages showing women and men what would be considered the proper ideal of beauty once the world came to an end.

'Did you and Benjamín think the same?'

'Benjamín could never give Cristina's body that intense

concentration. Love blurred his eyesight, cast a veil over her charms. Maybe that's why he clung on to her much more strongly, or maybe much more desperately. He was the best-looking of the three of us. As far as I was concerned,' he sighed, then went on, 'I could see beyond my love. I knew she was unique for me, but not the only one in the world. Even while I felt I could die for her, I knew that I wouldn't die for her. And she punished me for my impudence, for my lack of ignorance: she chose me as her confessor.'

'Just like Pesce.'

'I can assure you they are not the same,' he answered, a slight edge to his voice. 'Neither Guidi nor Benjamín knew that she was born a *goy*. She told me one evening in her house.

'Cristina had already been friends with Guidi and Benjamín for over a year. Guidi had had her in his room a couple of times, at the back of his parents' house. But you could hardly consider that a relationship. Benjamín pursued her hopelessly with the power of his intelligence. And I waited my turn, like one of those horses waiting for the donkey. Benjamín and I both took it for granted that the woman belonged first and foremost to Guidi. But Guidi never bothered in the slightest to assert his ownership. He boasted about having done it with the most beautiful woman in the world, but that fact never led him to set up any obstacles for anybody else.

'That time in her house...I stopped by to pick her up and take her to a party. There was a get-together in the house of one of Benjamín's cousins, just some friends coming round. I think there was a religious holiday coming up, Rosh Hashana maybe, and some friends were getting together before we celebrated it separately with our own families. I was already a great idiot and lived on my own. Cristina must have been about seventeen years old.

'That day she took me into her room where the light was dim, just the last evening light—did I talk to you about the evening light in Once?—that was coming in through the lowered slats of the blinds. Cristina was already the exuberant woman you have seen for yourself. But that evening she reached a level of beauty that she never reached again.

'She had dark rings under eyes and her body seemed to have shrunk a little. You could see she was eaten up with some sadness. She was the most beautiful woman in the world and about to fall apart: is there any jewel more precious than a unique one about to break apart because of some inner tension? For those moments just before this strange breaking apart, that jewel is the most valuable in the world: in a few seconds' time there will be nothing like it.

'Cristina was already the prettiest girl in the world before that evening when she became fragile: well, you can imagine her when she was on the point of falling apart.

'Next to her, on the bed, there was a small packet, a wrapping of white paper, a *paquele* as they say in Yiddish. Her mother Miranda had spent a week trying to get the *leikaj* right, the honeycake.'

'I know what *leikaj* is,' I said.

'She never managed,' Traúm went on. 'It was still edible, though. It looked like a chocolate cake without tasting of chocolate. It was insipid, but not offensive.

'Cristina's leg was trembling next to the packet. As it trembled the air around her trembled too, and the shifting air transmitted to the world the news of her beauty and her helplessness. Thousands of horsemen must have put on their spurs and polished their helmets, sharpened their swords and instructed their followers. But I got there before any of them: Elías, the oldest of the three musketeers.

'She took my hand and placed it on her left breast, and letting her head fall on my shoulder, she said in a whisper:

'"My daddy's dead."

'I've always believed, ever since the age of reason, that women who are excessively beautiful have a certain tendency to go mad. I don't know why. But Hollywood shows I'm right. Why this intuition? I don't know. Maybe an excess of beauty is worse than an excess of talent, less manageable. A body that is always and forever provoking reactions and the gaze of others. But I'm talking rubbish.

'The only thing I can tell you for sure is that even today this same intuition stays with me, though I can't explain it. That evening I thought Cristina had gone mad, or that she was mad, and that I shouldn't take advantage of her madness to do with her what I had wanted to do ever since I first laid eyes on her.

'Her father had come down to let me in and then he had left. There was no way he had died and no way, even if there was the faintest chance he had died in those minutes between me seeing him and Cristina bursting into tears, that she could have found out about it.

'No, Dr Torchinsky—sorry, B.A.Hons—hadn't died.

'"I've just seen him, Cristina," like someone waking a child from a nightmare with soothing words.

'"My daddy's dead," Cristina repeated, sobbing against me.

'I held her silently, rocking her gently and telling her it wasn't true.

'"I'm a *goy*," she said all of a sudden, in a loud and strong voice, her sobs stopping for a moment only to redouble uncontrollably.

'I held her away from me for a moment, I looked at her face. I had no more fear of taking advantage of her. Her delirium had banished my sexual tension.

'"I'm a *goy*,' she said again. "Torchinsky isn't my dad. My dad was a *goy*. And my mum is a converted *goy*. My dad died of cirrhosis of the liver, yesterday. I can't go to the party with you all. I don't know what to do, how to say good-bye to him. Should I pray to Christ? You lot don't have prayers for the dead for women to say. Tell me what I should do. How should I get to the cemetery? What do I wear?"

'And with no more tears she dropped back onto the bed and stretched out there, her eyes open but without looking at me, she told me the whole story. When she finished, I realised my hand was still on her left breast, where she had put it.'

There were still a few drops of black sticky liquid at the bottom of Traúm's glass, like something solid that had melted slightly, but it was hard to tell if it was the Pepsi or the Fernet, if indeed the two liquids can separate again once they've been mixed together.

'What did you do?' I asked.

'I took advantage of her,' Traúm answered without moving. 'I was the second musketeer to have her. That evening, in the fading light of her bedroom. She was covered by half darkness and what was left of the fragile light. We can't have taken long because we still got to the party in time. The *leikaj*, like I told you, was not too bad.'

The waiter asked us if we wanted anything else.

'If in the other world I'm allowed to repeat just one moment of my life,' said Traúm, 'I'll choose that one.'

Chapter twenty-four

Supposedly writing a feature piece on Traúm was beginning to get to me. I didn't want to let him go, but I tried to talk about anything other than his story. I really tried.

The business about Cristina made me sadder than I could bear. I couldn't see any connection between the trembling adolescent and the haughty mare I'd passed by in the the newspaper offices. For me the woman in Traúm's story was simply a young princess in danger whom I would like to have rescued.

I had long conversations with Traúm about Israel, not just in an effort to distract him from his epic and decidedly tragic friendship with Cristina, but because I was genuinely interested in the country of the Jews. What were the cities like, Jerusalem, Tel Aviv, Haifa? How did people live there? Could the Jews, at last, walk safely along the street?

I left Traúm at his hotel around one o'clock in the morning after listening to one of the most interesting and rational sociopolitical expositions of the Middle East that I had ever heard. Traúm turned out to be more than an expert on the region, he was also realistic and moderate. He had resigned himself to accepting the fact that people were not normal, and to stop trying to plan some sort of life based on that one certainty.

Nobody was watching us.

I went back home by taxi.

The whisky had completely gone, both the immediate effects and the consequent hangover. My head was intact but insomniac. Lying down on my bed, looking at what was left in the bottle of whisky as you might look at a chaste woman, I couldn't sleep.

I switched on the radio. I don't know what station it was tuned to, but the presenters seemed determined to shout and yell cheerfully even at that unlikely hour of the morning. The presenter had announced a riddle to the airwaves, one of those mind games that come in little books with the answers printed at the back.

The riddle involved two men, a woman, a murder, and was unsolvable. At least, it was not going to be solved over the course of the programme.

Nonetheless, after just five minutes a listener called up with the right answer.

The presenter allowed herself a few seconds of surprise and silence—most unusual in presenters—and finally exclaimed in an astonished voice:

'That's the right answer!'

And after another moment's silence she went back to her normal vacuousness with a false laugh of relief:

'Oh, you're a rascal, you are!' she said to the listener, whose voice announcing the answer to the riddle had disappeared from the airwaves. 'You had the book. You told us the answer using exactly the same words as the answer in the book. You cheated, but we're on to you! Right, let's have another riddle.'

I switched off the radio and lay there thinking about that listener. Did the world exist at that time of night? Wasn't it in the early hours of the morning, especially that most imprecise of hours, when we must all realise that we were not real, that we were projections, holograms created by crazed gods? Whatever the truth of that, I found myself thinking of the listener as if he was real. Why had he given out the answer from the book? Why had he bothered to call if he had the book anyway? The programme wasn't giving anything away, there were no prizes for the person who phoned with the correct answer. What possible purpose was served by struggling to get through on the phone to speak to a presenter whose mental faculties were in a serious state of disrepair, to be heard by truck drivers and night watchmen as he read out an answer printed at the back of a book?

No, I couldn't work it out. This was a riddle but there was no answer on the back of anything. I looked at the label on the whisky bottle.

The truth, I said to myself. The listener wanted to speak the truth. He had it within his grasp, and he simply felt the temptation to say it.

Traúm wanted to speak the truth. Pesce wanted to speak the truth. Cristina wanted to speak the truth, that evening when she was seventeen years old. Human beings have a tendency to speak the truth. Because there is a truth that is not relative, and that does not change. And our being yearns to seek it out and speak it when we come across it. And when we come across it, and when we speak it, we discover that it does nothing for us. And it doesn't make us happier, and it doesn't make us more at peace. There is no benefit and no reward. Truth does not perpetuate love and it does not save lives. It has no purpose.

So, why had the listener called?

I switched the radio back on and mentally assigned the presenter a sexual punishment for every idiotic statement that came out of her mouth. They were all variations on the act of sodomy.

I fell asleep.

Chapter twenty-five

When I woke I found I was aroused sexually. I didn't remember having any dreams that could have aroused me, but then I didn't need them. At times I just came back to the world of the living with a single need; to fuck.

Non-reproductive fucking is one of the activities in which the disproportion between the imagination leading up to the act and the concrete act itself and its consequences is greatest. An architect takes pleasure in his majestic and long-lasting building, a doctor sees in his living patient the long-lasting result of his work. But what transcendental reward is there for non-reproductive fucking? The only reward is the liberation from desire, accepting the useless impulses of one's spirit so as afterwards to be able to read, chat and drink like everyone else. Despite all that, before this moment of release the non-reproductive lovemaker constructs palaces of flesh, cities of skin, he envisions coitus as a work of art in which the material to be worked is his sweet victim. What limits are there to the imagination of the non-reproductive lovemaker? He will open up his lady from all sides, he will deploy her from her mouth to the soles of her feet, he will go from the bizarre to the cruel.

But in the future nothing more awaits him than his appeased desire. He will find no pleasure in everything he has imagined, he will feel a sense of disgust for everything that until a few moments ago he considered real pleasure.

I swallowed all the cups of tea my desperation allowed me and went out, thinking of Esther. I had to see her. I had to beg her to forgive me. I had to go to bed with her one more time.

I got on the first bus heading towards my old house. It was only just past ten o'clock in the morning, but it was already full. I had to be careful not to bump into anybody.

'Buy yourself a prostitute,' a wiser voice said to me. 'The state you're in, you'll frighten Esther. If you empty yourself into a prostitute you'll be able to let a bit of time go by and maybe Esther will come to forgive you.'

I saw the absolute sense of this line of reasoning, but I couldn't put it into practice.

I walked down to the back of the bus hoping at least to get somewhere near an open window. I stood near an old man, a fat woman and another woman armed with a plastic bag from a supermarket. The woman's bag was almost resting on the feet of another woman who was sitting down, holding her six- or seven-year-old son by the hand. The boy was staring out of the window.

As I stood trying to gulp in a little fresh air, I noticed the woman's buttocks. The bag somehow concealed the sight of our lower regions and hid a friction that seemed to come about of its own accord, I don't know how. Was it the inertia of the bus, or the unleashed desire of the woman with the shopping bag? Or maybe my will was overwhelmed by my own body?

I didn't make the slightest move to maintain contact, but the rubbing continued. As I was still trying to gasp for some air out of the window I saw that the boy, still holding his mother's hand, was watching us. Or rather, he was watching me.

Even though I knew this rubbing against each other was not down to me, I couldn't help feeling a certain sense of responsibility in the face of the boy's gaze, a slight cloud of shame.

What would be the consequences for this child of witnessing

acts defined as socially unacceptable? Would he remember my face simulating a calm and tranquil expression, pretending to be interested in what passed before my eyes outside the window? Would my poorly disguised lasciviousness come to haunt his adolescent nightmares?

'It's not my fault,' I said to myself. 'I'm not moving, I'm standing absolutely still. I haven't tried to move any closer to her. I'm just standing here in my place.'

The woman was wearing a white top and under the straps were two solid shoulders with some freckles. Her backside was glued to my trousers. She was wearing shorts of some rough material.

She was moving rhythmically, from one side to the other, and I knew that if I didn't move away the situation could get awkward for both of us. But standing there meant I could go on past the stop of my old house—now Esther's house—without getting off the bus. And so I closed my eyes and began to pray. I heard the woman breathing more heavily. Twenty blocks now separated me from Esther. I opened my eyes and saw the woman's twisted smile, the tense knuckles of her fist. She got off the bus without looking at me. I carried on watching her, but she didn't even turn round.

A bearded man went over to her on the pavement, a few steps away from the bus stop. He gave her a welcoming hug and kissed her on the cheek.

I got off at the next stop. An old man sitting near the window watched me.

I had to do something with myself. I refused to go into the the toilet of a bar and masturbate myself there. What if a homosexual walked in and heard me groaning? I took the first taxi that came by, and in a strange tone of voice gave my own address as if it belonged to somebody else.

It wasn't more than twenty minutes since I had left my flat, but I felt as if I was coming back from vacation in hell. I went to the bathroom and dropped my trousers. I couldn't even touch myself.

I left my trousers in the bathtub, scuttled to my bed and fell onto it. An unexpected, purely sexual energy—I wasn't even capable of getting off the bed—prompted me to see to myself one more time.

I didn't seek it out but the image of the woman in the bus came back into my mind.

Maybe I was like Pesce? Was I a monster too? No, it was the woman who had grabbed my attention. Her daring, her perversity. Imagination does no harm, I thought to myself. What about political writings? Ideas don't lead to actions, I told myself. Men act like beasts and then they seek out ideas to justify what they have done. Books are written to justify age-old actions, they do not provoke them. My last image, same as always, was of Esther. Now I was free, and I was destroyed.

I felt like an animal, something like a rat, damp with an unwholesome dampness.

'If I don't get off my bed now,' I said to myself, 'they'll find me here tomorrow, dead.' I glanced at *The War of the Jews*, whose spine was sticking out of the bookcase slightly, and asked the zealots for strength.

'Give me courage, men of Eleazar,' I begged silently. 'Allow me to die with you.'

But I did not want to die. There was a message on my answering machine.

It was Pesce, asking me to call him.

Chapter twenty-six

Supposedly, Pesce wanted me to 'cover' the Coast. I'd managed to get through to him after three concerts of *La cucaracha*. The very fact that I had managed finally to get through to him meant that he was waiting for me.

'Covering the Coast' meant spending a fortnight in a crap hotel in Mar del Plata, eating in a crap restaurant and inventing dialogues with fishermen, tourists and businessmen.

Three years before I had suggested to Pesce, after 'covering the Coast,' that we stop this farce and just reprint the same features every year.

'Like the magazines of Isidoro Cañones,' I said, 'we change the dates and prices, and we repeat the same stories. Read the summer features of the last fifteen years and tell me if there's a difference between any of them.'

On this occasion Pesce had to agree with me that, except for the death of the comedian Alberto Olmedo, we could have published the same coverage from 1983 onwards, just changing dates and prices.

But the newspaper had carried on sending journalists there each and every summer.

Not everyone invented dialogue like I did. Some of them really did ask tourists if the sun was very hot, the fishermen if there were any fish and the clients if they were happy with the prices they had to pay.

Pesce was informing me that once more I was to be the envoy charged with establishing this essential communication between those who were enjoying the seaside and those who were sweating on the tarmac back in the city.

'But señor Pesce,' I said to him, 'I was enjoying my leave.'

The sentence was weak, being neither normally colloquial nor part of my habitual satire mode. This is what happened to me when I behaved normally instead of making things up.

'It was me who came up with the leave, to protect you,' he said openly. 'Now you have to go and work on the Coast.'

'I don't enjoy the sun,' I told him. 'And my audiologist forbade me to put my head under water because of my ear infection. What am I supposed to do in Mar del Plata?'

'Work,' said Pesce. 'There's no point arguing. Come here this evening and pick up your tickets.'

'I'll come this evening to argue about it,' I said. 'You can't give me leave and then take it away from me just like that.'

But I knew they could do just that, and I also knew I would do more or less anything the paper told me to. I didn't want to lose my job. For the moment it was the only one I had.

I hung up and immediately called Traúm.

They were sending me to Mar del Plata just for the fun of it, or so I could bring them back a stick of rock. Pesce was scared.

It wasn't enough for them to keep me on ice. They wanted me out of town. What was going on?

The receptionist told me Traúm wasn't in his room. I asked her to check if he was maybe having lunch in the dining room. The receptionist said no, he wasn't, and no, she hadn't seen him go out.

'Did he sleep in his room last night?' I asked.

'I can't give out that kind of information,' she answered.

I left my name and rang off. I called my mother.

'Do you know where he is?' I asked her.

'He called an hour ago to say he wouldn't make it for lunch after all,' she said.

'Were you going to have lunch together?' I asked, alarmed.

'Yes,' she told me, and added thoughtfully 'But I don't suppose I'm the only one.'

'Mum,' I said to her, 'how can you talk to me like that?'

'It's a joke,' she said. And we both hung up.

I didn't dare ask her if she had any idea where Traúm might have spent the night.

It was eleven o'clock in the morning and even at this early hour I had drained any sense of meaning from my life—I didn't want to read, I didn't want to drink. Sex neither. I wasn't hungry and I didn't want to see a film. I felt a peculiar taste in my mouth and breathing was uncomfortable. We humans ask the State to provide us with work. And God we ask to tell us what to do with our lives.

If death were a state we could come back from, I'm sure a number of people would opt for that on occasion. Not me—I don't even take a siesta because it's only the dead who sleep during the day. But if they made me salesman for temporary death, I could offer it as a solution with more going for it than sleep, since when you're dead you don't suffer nightmares and you're not worried about wasting time. Nor do you run the risk of being woken up before your time.

The phone rang and I answered it halfheartedly. It was the first time in months I didn't leap on the phone as an animal pounces on its favourite dinner.

It was Gladis. An obesely fat schoolteacher I had mistreated a few years before getting together with Esther, and who I had started to mistreat again a few months after splitting up. I couldn't believe the things she had allowed me to do.

Each time we met I let her into the house and told her I had to go out. I asked her to iron my clothes, wash the dishes and scrub the floor.

'When I come back,' I would say to her, 'I want you to be there on all fours.'

Sometimes she squeaked a mild protest:

'I'd rather be standing so I can see your face.'

She was a virgin and she called herself the 'old spinster.' In thirty years on the face of this earth, her most significant sexual experience was to have been kissed in the dark by a physics teacher, whose impotence meant he couldn't possess her.

'He didn't even want to kiss my breasts,' Gladis confessed to me, weeping, 'he said they scared him.'

I, on the other hand, drove into her with neither patience nor compassion. On all fours, after she had done my washing and ironing.

'No,' I answered as she raised that small objection, 'you don't have any experience. Let me explain it to you. A woman, a real woman, obeys her man. It's not good that you see my face when I possess you—it shows a lack of respect.'

She bowed her head, submissive and happy, and pressed her face against the floor.

'She's happy,' a colleague at the paper said to me when I vented my feelings in a crisis of remorse. 'Do you hit her, do you force her, is she tied to you in any way?'

'She comes when she wants and she leaves when she wants,' I answered.

'In that case she's doing what she wants,' Liliana told me. 'But be careful,' she warned me. 'A woman who submits herself like that doesn't just walk away. She's going to ask you for something, something as bad as the humiliation you're putting her through. If you don't hit her and you don't force her, she'll be looking for some kind of exchange, some kind of deal. Have no doubt that she's going to give you the bill any time now, with the price underlined.'

And indeed, a few months after the start of my sordid paradise with Gladis, after a night in which I had drunkenly taken her I wasn't quite sure where or how, I asked her if I had been careless in any way.

'I don't know,' she told me.

'What do you mean you don't know?' I asked her, irritated and horrified by my own vulgarity.

'I don't know,' she repeated. 'I don't have any experience. But if I get pregnant I'm going to keep it.'

'You're crazy,' I told her.

'I wouldn't have an abortion for anything in the world,' she told me in a tone that was threatening in its sweetness.

I spent a couple of nights of sleepless desperation. Finally destiny revealed that I had not strayed from the usual safe path offered by doing it on all fours.

But while I was relieved, I swore I would never see her again. Liliana was right: a man like me couldn't keep up a relationship of this kind without running more of a risk than his apparently unfortunate consort.

After Esther left me, my promises fell by the wayside. Esther had walked away from me and taken these decisions with her. I no longer had any respect even for myself.

I'd met Gladis in the street and taken her back to my bachelor flat. Her face still looked like a cow's and her arse wasn't quite yet sufficiently autonomous to disgust me. She carried on washing the floor and the dishes. But I was careful not to get drunk before using her.

I told her 'no' on the phone this time. I didn't need her. I promised myself to do without her forever.

Somehow or other time dragged itself round to three o'clock in the afternoon. Time can be merciful—it just goes on by.

And it had moved far enough on for me to justify a trip to the newspaper office to discuss my business with Pesce.

I showered and recovered something of my dignity. I even shaved and put some aftershave lotion on. What was the lotion for? Some people claimed it was to relieve the irritation left on the skin by the scraping of the razor blades. But my face burnt more with the lotion than without it. Others reckoned it was to stop the itching. But my face itched more half an hour after using the lotion. As Maugham said: 'it was a riddle that shared with the universe the merit of having no answer.'

I left the flat hoping not to break into a sweat, and took a taxi. Perspiration is a liquid which we humans have not learnt to withhold.

Fabiana greeted me with a distinct coldness, hovering somewhere between fear and disapproval. As if they had forced her to be polite to a giant cockroach.

'Señor Pesce told me you are to wait in reception,' she said as she dialled the extension.

'I'll go through to his office,' I said.

'In reception,' she repeated firmly.

On the phone she said sweetly that there was someone waiting in reception, without saying my name.

I wasn't allowed past reception. This wasn't looking good.

Pesce came towards me with a large envelope in his hand.

'Let's go out for a walk,' he said.

We went out and walked along the narrowest stretch of Calle Bartolomé Mitre.

'It's not enough for them that you are on leave,' Pesce told me. 'They went mad. They want you completely out of the way.'

'What is it you are talking about, señor Pesce?'

He gave me the envelope without saying a word. He stopped, and I had to retrace a few steps.

'Can you tell Elías to leave?' he asked me.

'I've already told him that.'

'You've got two tickets there for Mar del Plata, two returns. At least you could take him to Mar del Plata with you.'

'I don't know where he is,' I said.

'Since when?'

'Since last night.'

'This is beyond me,' said Pesce, and his face was pale.

'Is it that bad?' I asked.

'Completely beyond me,' repeated Pesce, beaten. 'Don't you two ever learn? Are you determined to go out looking for a killer? Why don't you stay in?'

'You gave me this feature to do, señor Pesce,' I said.

'I didn't know. How could I know that Elías would annoy Ruiz Reches. Why do the two of you piss off the whole world? Do you want another murder? How many are going to be left, five?'

'Who's you?' I asked finally.

'The Jews,' Pesce answered, as he turned on his heel and walked quickly away.

Chapter twenty-seven

I had no intention of going to Mar del Plata and I didn't know where Traúm was.

Where was Traúm anyway? Had death come back with no mitigating circumstances? Were they torturing him, did they have him locked in a filthy hole somewhere, in a clandestine prison, half 'people's prison', half jail to the aristocracy? Had Ruiz Reches been sent into a rage, afraid that all of Argentina would know about the triple sexual relationship with the three musketeers, while feeling untouchable enough to contemplate tossing out onto the side of the road the body of a dead Jew who hadn't wanted to go back to Mosesland?

Anything could have happened. And not because we were in the twentieth century: simply because we were on the planet Earth, amongst members of the human race.

I started to feel desperate. Traúm was either dead or suffering the most dreadful torture. Every trace of good humour disappeared from my thoughts. I didn't even care about my own life.

I called the hotel once more. Señor Traúm had not been back to his room. A shaft of light struck me and I called my mother.

'Mother,' I said to her. 'I have a couple of free tickets to Mar del Plata to give you. You can go with a friend.'

'Ah, darling,' she said. 'I must have done something good for you to give me things like that. But I can't at the moment.'

'You're on holiday, though. Have a few days away in Mar del Plata. You love walking along the Rambla there. Go with Sara, or with Mary.'

'I can't, son. I have a lot to do here in Buenos Aires. Señor Traúm called me today to ask my pardon.'

'Today?' I shouted.

'Yes, today,' said my mother, taken aback. 'Today we can use the phone. It's not the Sabbath and it's not Yom Kippur. He said he wouldn't be able to come by today, but that he'll be in touch soon.'

'Did he leave you a phone number?'

'No, but I've got the hotel number.'

'Do you really not want to go to Mar del Plata?'

'Really,' said my mother. 'Why don't you ask Esther?'

'We're separated, mother.'

'Mar del Plata is the place for reconciliation.'

He wasn't dead. Or maybe he was. It was perfectly possible that he had a few words with my mother just before a bullet hit him in the back of the neck. Without going too far from home, my father had asked my mother for a bookmark for his five-hundred page book— I can't remember if it was Ira Levin or Leon Uris—and at that very moment he died of a heart attack. I had no reason to discard any of my worst suspicions.

Where was Traúm? Why was it he couldn't today? I didn't care anymore if there was anything going on between Traúm and my mother. I only wanted them both to be safe. There was nothing I could do. Desperation clouded my brain. If I didn't call Esther I would fall down dead on the spot, amidst all the passersby, leaning against the public phone box.

She answered.

'There's no sign of Traúm,' I said. 'I fear the worst. I have to see you.'

'Come on over,' she said.

She was still being my wife, my guardian angel, my practicing Jew.

As I went up in the elevator past the third and fourth floor, I saw some writing on the walls, graffiti in red spray paint.

'Have the henchmen been here?' I wondered, 'have they been writing anti-Semitic stuff in my old building? Will they kill Esther because of me?'

She let me in, gave me some iced tea and let me sit down heavily on the sofa.

'What are all those inscriptions on the walls on the third and fourth floor?' I asked her, terrorised.

'The transsexual on the third floor is threatening to kill the dancer on the fourth floor,' said Esther.

'That whore Mario?'

'Don't call him that.'

Mario was a third-rate dancer and I was sure he was being kept by a series of boyfriends who, even more strangely, used to wait for him downstairs in the entrance with bunches of flowers, bottles of champagne or simply a leather jacket and dark glasses. The transsexual from floor three was a blonde giantess who took up half the elevator, always in work clothes at nighttime and with an inscrutable expression on her face. I was afraid of her.

'I don't know what they fell out about,' said Esther. 'But the transsexual got a spray can and wrote that Mario's got AIDS.'

I held my head in my hands, fell back and sighed in relief. It wasn't the Nazis.

'What's that sigh for?' asked Esther.

'There are worse things,' I said.

I told her in detail about what was happening with Traúm and what I was afraid of.

'Just for once,' said Esther, 'you're right to be afraid. Why don't you go to Mar del Plata? You can't do anything here. Maybe if you leave they'll calm down.'

'If you come with me,' I said.

Esther looked at me, annoyed. She was silent for a few moments and finally she said:

'I have to leave. If you want you can have a siesta here. But I'd prefer you not to be here when I get back.'

'Agreed,' I said.

Maybe my mother was right and Mar del Plata was the place for reconciliation. But Esther was refusing to go and walk along the Rambla. I was lost.

As soon as she left I headed for the cheap piece of furniture where we kept our drinks and took out the whisky. It was still exactly where we'd left it, meaning it hadn't been offered to anyone else. I poured myself a generous amount, paying careful attention to the level in the bottle. I drank it sitting down on the chair. I stood up again and poured myself another shot. I took note of the level again. I drank this glass lying down, and fell asleep. I was woken soon after by the phone ringing.

I answered because I was still asleep, because I'd forgotten that Esther wasn't with me and that this wasn't my house. If that hadn't been the case, in all honesty I would never have picked up the phone.

'Señor Mossen?' asked a mellifluous voice.

Was this perhaps one of the henchmen?

'Who is speaking?' I asked, trying futilely to impart a note of authority to my voice which was fuzzy with sleep.

'My name is Giancarlo Buossini.'

'Buossini?' I repeated.

'The father of Mario Buossini.'

Mario Buossini was the dancer from the fourth floor.

'Ah,' I said.

'I imagine you are aware of the nightmare my son is being put through?'

'I know about it by pure chance,' I said.

'You are a writer, aren't you?' he asked.

'Journalist,' I said.

'But you write for a newspaper, don't you?'

'Most of the time my pieces don't carry my name.'

'But do you write or don't you?'

'No, the truth is that I don't write,' I said. 'I just deal with putting bits and pieces together.'

'Fine, that's a newspaper,' said Giancarlo Buossini. 'You must know about the law against discrimination. That woman is interfering with my son's private life.'

That woman was the transsexual.

'She is broadcasting intimate details of my son's life to the four winds. And that, sir, is punishable by law. Illness is not a crime, but persecution is.'

'And why are you telling me all this?' I asked.

'You are a journalist. You know about the law. I imagine you get involved in this sort of thing. I don't have the slightest wish to take any legal action against this woman. But if she leaves us no option we will take her to court. Can I take it that we can count on you? I've heard very good things about you.'

'I don't live here anymore, señor Buossini. You should direct your complaint to the administrators, they will know what to do.'

'The administrators say it is a problem that the neighbours will have to sort out between themselves. Do you know how this quarrel began?'

'No, señor Buossini, and I'm not much interested. I don't live here anymore.'

'Why?' he asked.

'The newspaper is sending me to Bahía Blanca for a year. I'm just calling by today. My plane leaves in an hour and a half.'

'Hurry up or you'll miss it,' he told me. 'Can we count on you then?'

'What for?'

'The business between my son and that woman.'

'No,' I said. 'It's really backward in Bahía Blanca. Who gave you my phone number?'

'The doorman. I knew you were a writer.'

We hung up by mutual agreement, after señor Buossini expressed his gratitude for my listening and repeated his belief that he could 'count on me.'

I realised I was dizzy and bleary. It wasn't so much a hangover as the alcohol made worse by having my sleep interrupted. I seriously contemplated suicide. I was afraid I didn't know how to carry on living. It was seven in the evening and I had to get out of my ex-wife's house. I called Gladis. She lived in Lugano Uno. I asked her if she wanted to see me.

She said yes straight away and promised to make me a chocolate cake.

I had to do something.

I called a taxi. It arrived in five minutes and I gave the driver Gladis's address. On the way I tapped my hand against the envelope which held the tickets, and made up dirty rhymes about Gladis and Lugano.

Chapter twenty-eight

Gladis welcomed me on all fours. With her face pressed against the floor and the cake in the fridge. I consented to fulfil the request suggested by her physical position like a careful owner. My sexual senses were fully functioning.

Then I didn't want to see her anymore, even sooner than I expected. I stayed a few more minutes to have a taste of the chocolate cake. I ate half of it. I was profoundly depressed, and Lugano Uno and Lugano Dos were not the best therapy.

'Don't go,' begged Gladis. 'Won't you kiss me?'

'It wouldn't be right,' I said. 'We are not husband and wife.'

'What's that got to do with it?' she said. 'We do things that are much worse.'

'No,' I said. 'What we do is much less intimate than a kiss. That's why I do it, so things don't get too intimate between us. If we are going to kiss we have to decide where our relationship is going.'

'Kiss me,' Gladis asked. And she shed a tear.

Liliana was right. Gladis handed me a bill at the end of every day. She was a kind of secret mafiosa type who never gave out favours without asking them back later.

I kissed her against my will and felt sick. She smelt of cough syrup.

'There you go,' I said.

'My life has no sense,' said Gladis.

'Whose does?'

'You're strong, powerful,' Gladis said to me. 'I'm disgusting, aren't I?'

'Who told you that?' I said. 'You've got a great body. Didn't you see how you excite me?'

'You don't even let me look at you.'

'Because that's how it is between a man and a woman,' I said. 'The thing is, you have no experience.'

'You turn up when you want. Sometimes I want to die.'

'Ours is an informal relationship,' I said. 'You have to let many years go by before you can decide what type of relationship it is. Otherwise you can make terrible mistakes.'

'You despise me. I don't care if I live or die.'

'Gladis,' I said, 'I brought you a present. But if you go on talking like that I'm not going to give it to you.'

'A present?' she asked, brightening up straight away.

'A present for my little seal,' I said.

'What is it?' asked Gladis.

'Lie down on the floor and clap like a seal,' I said to her kindly.

She did.

'Here you are,' I said.

I gave her one of the tickets to Mar del Plata.

'A ticket to Mar del Plata!' she shouted.

'For my little seal,' I said.

'Are you coming?' she asked me.

'I can't, I have work to do. But I bought it especially for you.'

'I don't believe it.'

'For my little seal.'

'You're divine,' said Gladis. 'Will you come if you've got time?'

'Of course. I'll turn up in the Bristol Hotel all of a sudden.'

Gladis turned around, left the ticket on the floor and started clapping like a seal again, waving her hips in front of me.

'Do you want to do it with me as if I were a seal?' she asked me.

'Fine,' I said.

On my way back—another taxi—I felt fear once more for Traúm's fate. They'd killed him while I was playing seals with Gladis. Or worse: they'd killed him because I had been playing seals with Gladis. If someone behaves in a particularly frivolous way during a period of time when a tragic situation might come about, he makes that tragedy much more likely to happen. God sees all and applies his judgement. How could I have been playing seals with that whale of a woman while they were about to murder one of my brothers?

Unfairly, I hated Gladis even more than I hated myself.

I saw her clapping on the floor, and I wanted her to die. Afterwards I took that back: her neighbours in Lugano had seen me going in and out of her house: if she died for some reason it would cause me a problem. I asked God why she didn't kill herself. It was true that when I left her horrible apartment she was as happy as a small animal, but her seal-like cheer didn't wipe out the suicidal tendencies that whales were prone to.

Physical weariness didn't go hand in hand with any sense of relief.

The depression I felt was lifting, but only to be replaced by anxiety and fear. If there was no message from Traúm when I got home, I was going to call the Israeli embassy. After all, Traúm was an Israeli citizen. Israel wouldn't let him down.

I went up to my apartment, my decision made. I opened the door and looked at the answering machine without switching the light on. No messages. Now it was a question of finding the phone directory and calling. But it was ten o'clock at night, who would be at the embassy at this time of night, Golda Meir?

Somebody switched on the light in the sitting room of my rented apartment. I cried out, loudly. I cried out like a woman, like a monster, like a malignant doll. It was a hysterical, terrified cry, but full of power. The cry of the zealot when he receives death at the hand of a brother.

Before me stood the spectre of Traúm. I saw him hanging from the ceiling, like a news editor hanged in the offices of the Communist Party during the military dictatorship. I saw him covered in blood, riddled with bullets, tossed into the woods around the airport inside a nylon bag like the assassins of the Peronist right during Perón's last government. I saw him pale and skeletal like the survivor of a concentration camp.

But he was alive and in one piece, with natural colour and a trusting smile.

'I know how to open doors and break in,' he said. 'Sorry.'

Chapter twenty-nine

Where did you learn how to get into people's houses like a thief?' I asked him.

'Not like a thief, no,' said Traúm thoughtfully. 'Like the prophet Elías.'

'I hope you haven't been helping yourself to my whisky.'

'I only drink what's left out for me. Are you coming with me on my nighttime walk?'

'I thought you were dead or being tortured. Where were you, what happened?'

'I had breakfast early, out of the hotel. I wanted the traditional milky coffee and brioche in a bar, and in the hotel you can't help feeling like a foreigner. I went back for a shower and in the doorway I saw the two cretins who robbed me on the motorway. They were just a few steps away from the janitor and I thought, what can they do to me here, in broad daylight with the whole world looking on? But I didn't want to take any chances. In the worst period for the three musketeers I learnt how to be anonymous in the city. I know how to hide. I called your mother.'

'I know that,' I said, hoping that the brevity of my answer

would suggest there was nothing about my mother that I did not know.

'Are you coming with me?'

'I thought I was going to have to go and identify your body in the morgue. No walk can be worse than that. Where do you want us to go at this time of night?'

'To Benja's house.'

'Your friend Benjamín?'

'The youngest of the three musketeers.'

'How did you find it?'

'Cristina told me.'

'Cristina?'

'Our queen.'

'But isn't she the one who wanted you out of here? Pesce practically extradited me to Mar del Plata.'

'My impression is that it's not our powerful Cristina who's after us—not in this eloquent manner, at least. Cristina might not want us here, but I don't think she'd make herself quite so unpleasant. It's the evil Richelieu who doesn't want us anywhere around on the day of his wedding.'

'How did Cristina get in touch with you to give you the address of Benjamín's house?'

'As well as your message, when I phoned the hotel they told me a woman had called but hadn't left her name. There was an address: Ecuador 1.322. I was worried it was a trap, but it was Benja's house. His mother is still living there.'

'But didn't you tell me you didn't know where your friends' families lived?'

'They told me she wasn't living there anymore. But she is. She's not well. Her mind's gone.'

'And are you sure it was Cristina who left the information?'

'She's the only one who could have known it.'

'What about Pesce, and all the possible ramifications there?'

'It's Cristina. She's the only one who would leave a message without her name.'

'You trust your intuition too much.'

'Intuition is the least fallible system we have for reaching knowledge.'

We went out. In the lift mirror I saw how pale my face was. You could still see in my face the fear of death that Traúm had induced in me.

Chapter thirty

First off, Traúm made me eat a steak with chips and fried eggs. We were headed along Ecuador and Tucumán, but in order to find a suitable place to eat we wandered towards the centre and found ourselves on Sarmiente, towards Callao.

'You don't get this in Israel,' he told me, dipping a chip in the runny egg yolk.

We washed it down with beer.

'You think you're the prophet Elijah, Elías,' I said to him. 'But if you carry on like that you'll turn into Father Christmas.'

'Can you think of anything more *goyish* than Father Christmas?' Traúm asked, inserting a small and shapeless piece of steak in a hollowed-out bread bun, which he had swabbed in the egg yolk left on the side of his plate.

'With that white beard he could be a rabbi,' he went on. 'Even so, as soon as you lay eyes on him you know he's a *goy*. Maybe because he's smiling,' he added.

'When I used to go to Mar del Plata with my parents,' I told Traúm, 'I often saw gigantic plastic Father Christmases, lit up from inside. They made me feel really happy.'

'Why didn't they go to Miramar for the summer?'

'It's not very Jewish to do everything by the book.'

'Variety in the world is a blessing from God,' said Traúm, and he asked for the bill with the typical gesture of a Buenos Aires resident.

'Do people ask for the bill like that all over the West?' I asked him.

'Of course not,' said Traúm. 'But they'll bring it for you anyway. Always.'

We reached Once at one in the morning. Calle Tucumán was protected by those harmless midges of summer nights, which look like mosquitoes but don't bite, and swirl around the light of the lampposts rather more cautiously than others of their species. The air was still and its warmth invited Man to remain down on earth. Finally the planet seemed to be suited for its inhabitants. Human beings enjoyed the truce of sleep. I would have liked to look through the shutters of the single-story houses along Tucumán and Azcuénaga to see how all these strangers made love. Would there be a husband forcing his wife to submit to an act of impiety? Or a hefty matron jiggling indefatigably over a fat man on the verge of total collapse? A young man, a child almost, maybe pretending to sleep in his cousin's bed and pressing himself up against her? I imagined that at this time of night in this part of town everybody was asleep by now, but I was hugely curious about other people's intimacies, and I would have given anything for the gift of being able to get myself unseen inside all of these houses like a Father Christmas who, instead of leaving presents, steals away their secrets.

'Since Benja lived on Ecuador and Guidi here on Paso, on the Corrientes side, every time we went out, on the way back we would come together as far as that lamppost. It was the point more or less equidistant between our three houses.'

Traúm pointed to a lamppost we'd already passed about a block and a half back, in the middle of Tucumán, between Paso and Acuénaga.

'The same lamppost?' I asked.

'The same one,' said Traúm. 'Yes, it's strange to think that the two of them have died and the layout of the city hasn't changed. At least when there's a war on things get broken too.'

'Did they kill anybody?' I asked suddenly, without knowing why.

'Guidi and Benja?' he asked.

I nodded.

'I don't know,' said Traúm. 'But I think of them as murderers anyway. Murderers.'

'Your friends?' I asked.

'My dead friends,' said Traúm.

We'd reached Calle Ecuador. We were talking about two Jews in the district of Once, and it seemed more like a Greek tragedy. Traúm carried straight on down Tucumán and pointed out a scrap of wasteland. I followed him.

There were thistles and broken bottles. Real mosquitoes and excrement of various animals: dogs and horses.

'What are we doing here?' I asked him.

'We're going into Benja's house round the back.'

'Aren't they expecting you?'

'They're expecting me, but we can't ring the bell.'

'Like the prophet Elijah,' I said.

'It's for Benja's mother's sake,' said Traúm, climbing onto the metre-and-a-half high wall that separated the wasteland from the back of Benja's house. 'She's not well.'

Thank God, on the last stretch of wall there were none of those bits of glass along the top that are often placed there to keep people out. Was that an Argentinian invention? Traúm fell to the ground on the other side and a second or so later I landed beside him. Like two thieves.

The garden was neglected, with a small vine that had long overgrown.

Traúm wasn't even out of breath. His fifty years had taken this test of jumping and climbing with remarkable dignity. As for me, despite the fact that I didn't smoke I was panting like a wild boar.

I felt overweight, and through my clothes I had scraped the soft skin of my belly against the cement.

Traúm gestured to me to follow him, but he didn't raise a finger to his lips to indicate that we should be silent.

We took a few steps towards a sliding glass door.

The sky was full of stars, but seen from that garden it didn't look majestic. It was as if the section of the sky to be seen from there had been just as neglected and abandoned over the last twenty years.

Inside the house, the other side of the glass door, an elderly woman whose hair was done up in a bun was watching a subtitled film on the television with great attention. The upholstery of the chair she was sitting in was a vulgarly modern material that already looked old and battered. The carpet was threadbare. The walls were thrown into shadow by an ugly light coming from a weak bulb and were painted with a kind of artex that had been fashionable some time when I was a kid, and which in this environment had a yellowish tinge like rotting teeth.

Traúm knocked gently on the glass door with his fist and the woman got up to let us in, as if she'd been waiting for us.

'Is that the mother?' I asked.

'The aunt,' said Traúm.

The woman slid back the door and said to us:

'I'll go and get her. You wait here.'

She went back in, switched off the television and disappeared inside the house.

'If Teófila hears the bell, she says that Benja's not in. Whoever it is: it could be the postman, a friend or someone in the family. She says that Benja's not in and she asks them to leave. Or she just tells Raquel to show them to the door. That's why we came in round the back.'

'She'll throw us out anyway,' I said.

'I don't think so,' said Traúm. 'Shhh, they're coming.'

The glass door had stayed open and Teófila, Benja's mother, was following her sister like a guide dog, her hair tied up in an identical bun.

'Benja's not in,' said Teófila when she saw Traúm.

'I know,' said Traúm. 'I know.'

'He should be back by now,' said Teófila. 'He went out with his friends.'

Then Traúm said something that frightened me even more than his sudden appearance in my house.

'With Guidi?' he asked.

'And Elías, too,' said Teófila.

Although this conversation was, for me, just rather dreadful and pathetic, I spotted on Elías's face an expression close to a grimace. Raquel's eyes were watery and her face was strained and sad.

'Where did they go?' asked Elías.

'To Hebraica,' said the woman. 'For a conference, I think. He must be on his way back by now. Raquel, show these boys to the door. They can call back later, he must be almost back by now.'

'Let's do *kaddish* and then we'll go,' said Elías to Teófila.

'*Kaddish*? Who for?' asked Teófila, alarmed.

'For all our loved ones,' said Elías gently.

'Let's go into the house in that case,' said Raquel. 'We can't pray out in the open air.'

We went into the sitting room. Hanging over an old Formica sideboard full of bowls of sweets was, rather absurdly, a shiny picture of Lenin addressing the masses.

'I'll go and fetch *quipu*,' said Raquel as she exited the scene.

Teófila stood in front of us as if she didn't even see us, in the passive position of a blind man waiting for his guide to come back.

Next to the sideboard a small glass table groaned under cheap ornaments. Over that was a photo of Benjamín as a boy, one or two of the three musketeers, a photo of a landscape that looked like Galilee and a green-painted copper candelabra with Hebrew letters and the word 'Israel' in Latin letters.

'Benja's father was a communist,' Elías whispered in my ear, seeing my surprise at the picture of Lenin. 'He used to boast that Benja was born in this very room, under the gaze of the father of the Bolsheviks.'

'What about Guidi's house?' I whispered back, almost inaudibly. 'Were there pictures of famous revolutionaries there too?'

'No. Only one of his father's great-grandfather, a famous Lithuanian rabbi. Anti-hassidic.'

'What about in yours?' I asked.

'A photo of Dr Herzl,' Elías managed to reply just as Raquel returned with the two skullcaps.

One of the two, I supposed, had belonged to Benjamín. And as I put it on my head I feared that the destiny of Benjamín Janín would fall on my head as well.

'Do you know *kaddish*?' Elías asked me.

'I don't know any prayers at all,' I answered.

'Repeat what I say then,' Elías told me.

Elías began to pray in a monotone voice, Raquel followed him, slightly off, like an out-of-tune canon, and I tried to repeat the words of Elías. Teófila watched us in puzzled silence.

'I don't know what time he'll be back,' she said to us at the door. 'Call in an hour's time.'

She gave Elías a kiss—not me—and left Raquel to lock up behind us. She went back to her room.

'She thinks she'll be strong enough to wait for Benjamín until she dies,' said Raquel.

Chapter thirty-one

The voice startled us even before we reached Pueyrredón, on our way back to the centre. We thought we'd go back along Corrientes, because we'd already done Tucumán, passed down it like some sort of catharsis, and we didn't want to retrace our steps, muddying the soles of our shoes in leftover nostalgia and tragedy. At that time of night Tucumán was the smashed glass, to be left on the floor. But the voice, the cry, made us head back up Tucumán. It was Raquel. Had Benjamín come back? I thought. Had Teófila died from *kaddish*? Was the portrait of Lenin weeping or speaking?

'Telephone,' said Raquel to Elías.

It was two o'clock in the morning and for the second time that night, without ringing the bell, we went into the house of Teófila Janín, mother of Benjamín, the youngest of the three musketeers.

A large grey telephone, a very old model, was lying with its mouth facing upwards. I was even more astonished than Traúm.

'Teófila won't get up,' Raquel told me as Elías brought the phone to his ear, 'unless the doorbell rings.'

'*Ken*,' said Elías.

He was speaking Hebrew.

There followed about fifteen minutes' conversation in Hebrew, during which the only words I caught clearly was the word Guidi, followed by a long silence from Traúm.

He hung up and stood there with a far-off expression on his face, like someone who has just left his girlfriend, or like someone who has been granted the gift of being able to converse with a memory.

'Was it that slut?' asked Raquel.

Traúm nodded.

'Why does Raquel hate Cristina so much?' I asked Elías when we finally made it past Tucumán. Now, indeed, Corrientes was dead but luminous, and carried us along its prudent asepsis. Here there were no smells, no memories. The shops sold vulgar, cheap clothes, the names were left over from English, all with an apostrophe. Here sadness had no foothold and the past could find no way in.

'Jealousy,' Traúm told me.

'Jealous of Benjamín?' I asked disbelievingly. 'Jealous?'

'I started with Raquel,' Traúm said, putting an end to my questioning.

'In the physical sense of the word,' Traúm told me. 'Raquel was my first woman.'

'You had Benjamín's aunt?' I said, with a minimum of subtlety. 'But she's an old woman!'

'She can't be sixty-five yet,' Traúm told me. 'And she must still be hiding a nice bit of flesh under that bun.'

The shop windows along Corrientes, frivolous and showily lit up as they were, listened in silent amazement to this extraordinary and untimely confession. We reached Pasteur.

'When I was eighteen years old, she was a fine woman.'

'Was she married?' I asked.

'No,' said Traúm shortly. 'Everybody in the family was very worried because they hadn't got her married off. I'd gone to look for Benjamín—I had to take him to a Jewish institution where at the time he was the pupil and I was the teacher—and she was there visiting her sister. Benjamín was late getting back, like today. She told me that Benjamín was too intelligent, that I was older and I should look after him. And then she told me life was crap.'

'Why?' I asked.

'Because nobody in the family would leave her alone. They were going to force her to get married. She knew she wouldn't be able to hold out and she would have to get married.'

'Why didn't she want to get married?'

'She had a *goy* boyfriend, a rocker who was going nowhere, with his leather jacket. He came and went, and at that moment he wasn't around. She didn't dare introduce him to her parents.'

'What did you say to her?'

'I told her life wasn't easy for us guys either. That all my mates— except my friends Guidi and Benjamín—had started out with a whore or a servant. And I didn't want that for myself. But it wasn't easy.'

'Was it in that same house?' I asked.

'In Benjamín's bed,' said Traúm. 'Raquel had the whitest thighs in the world.'

'Is that good?' I asked.

'Of course,' said Traúm.

'And did she get married?'

'Never,' Traúm almost shouted out. 'I heard that she became very Jewish, studying a lot and all that. And later she joined a kind of sect run by a dissident rabbi, one of those rare beings. Generally those outlandish groups are always going on about the kabbalah. It's like the tarot for Jews who can't be bothered to study. I don't think Raquel lasted very long there, she was an attractive woman. If they hadn't gone on at her so much, she might have made a good marriage.'

'We're nearly at Callao,' I told Traúm. 'Where are you going to sleep?'

'In a small hotel somewhere,' said Traúm. 'They've lost track of me.'

'Did you leave all your things at your hotel?'

'The room is still in my name. This is great,' said Traúm. 'The husband is chasing us and the wife is trying to help us.'

'You're all crazy,' I said nervously, talking about the lot of them. 'This is all going to end in tears. The man's really annoyed, and he's really powerful. It's bad enough that you go tramping around here just a few days before the wedding. He's worried, and I don't blame him, that you're going to shoot your mouth off with a double-page colour spread in my paper, telling the world about how the three of you were having it off with his wife at the same time.'

'Do you really think I could do that, then?' he asked me.

'No, I don't,' I said. 'But your mere existence is a threat to him. Who knows, maybe he wants to kill you before they invent a machine that will preserve the memories of dead people. The poor man can't much fancy one day seeing the pornographic video taken from Traúm's memory with his wife in the leading role.'

'Traúm's memory,' said Traúm. 'It would be a metal box with a little piece of paper on it with a classification number. My body would be under the ground, but my memories would be alive in a metal box. Traúm's memory. Would you keep it?' he asked.

'I'm sure I would,' I said, without thinking.

'If you had that memory in your hands, and they were chasing you to hand it over, because they wanted to destroy it, would you run away with the box to keep it safe?'

'Yes,' I said.

Traúm laughed.

'I believe you,' he said then. 'Now I have to find a place to sleep.'

'Don't be so bloody stupid,' I replied. 'Come and sleep at my place.'

Traúm shook his head.

'Cristina,' I said, but without insisting. 'How does she know Hebrew?'

'She learnt it as a girl.'

'But she was already grown up when her mother separated. Hebrew is difficult.'

'She wanted to learn it,' said Traúm. 'The passion of the converted,' he added with a smile.

'Imagine her having it off with this man and she lets slip a word in Hebrew,' I said, without guarding my speech.

'In bed Cristina is like a forest fire: it doesn't matter if the branches are dry or green, they all catch fire, whatever language she speaks in…'

In this last, unfinished statement I felt a remnant of pain, of loss, or maybe the anxiety of lust. Maybe I had been merciless.

'Listen, Traúm,' I said. 'If you don't want to we won't sleep, but come to my house. You'd be welcome. The Bible's very clear on this—we have to offer shelter to the traveller. I'm not planning to wash your feet, but I've got some whisky and I make a decent cup of mate tea.'

'Ah well, if it's in the Bible,' said Traúm.

And we stopped a taxi.

'But you don't have to do everything that's in the Bible,' Traúm added seriously, after a long silence, when we had given the driver my address.

Chapter thirty-two

Only fear for Traúm's life could have induced me to offer to take him home with me. I hate sharing rooms or changing rooms. Ever since I stopped having to go to summer camps or other group activities, I've always done my best to avoid seeing other men either naked or in pyjamas. Working at the paper, though, had condemned me more than once to sharing a room with a photographer during trips for low-level work. This was the first time in my adult life I'd invited another man to spend the night under my roof. I don't like sleeping in other people's houses, and I don't like them sleeping in mine. It's only sex that makes it possible for two people to share their days without killing each other.

Traúm sat on my green beanbag as if it was a comfortable place to sit down. He took off his shoes.

'Maté tea or whisky?' I asked him

'Tea first,' he answered.

I put on the water and left it to itself. However much I watched over it, it usually boiled. I'd got used to forgetting it was on until the kettle was shaking it was boiling so hard, then leaving it with the lid off until the water cooled down a bit. Paradoxically I normally ended up drinking the tea cold. On this occasion, perhaps because I had a guest, I managed to get the water hot enough without boiling it on the first go.

Traúm tasted it and it seemed to go down all right.

On a tiny, old but decent wooden table next to the phone sat the envelope containing the remaining train ticket to Mar del Plata, silent witness to our conversation.

'This envelope has one of the two tickets Pesce gave me,' I said.

'Are you afraid of flying?' he asked me.

'Of course,' I said. 'Who isn't? But it's not a phobia, I'm just frightened it will fall out of the sky.'

'We could fly to Mar del Plata,' said Traúm.

'Do you want to see La Feliz again?'

'I've just been invited down there.'

'Cristina Sobremonte?'

'She wants to see me in the airport at Camet,' said Traúm, stretching and yawning like someone getting ready for sleep in a large double bed. 'Want to come?'

'I stayed in Buenos Aires so you wouldn't be left here on your own,' I said. 'And now you're going there.'

'What can I do? Bring you back a stick of rock? I'm inviting you.'

'When do we leave?' I asked.

'Tomorrow evening, on the last flight. My flight's already paid for. I'll pay for yours.'

I was afraid that after his last stretch Traúm would fall right asleep. Now he looked like a man capable of sleeping sitting up, or in any other position.

'Tell me what it was like, Traúm.'

'What what was like?'

'When you all had her at once.'

Traúm stayed stretched out, but his expression changed to that of someone resigned to having to get out of bed and interrupt his sleep because of an unexpected guest.

'Aren't we going to sleep?' he asked.

'Tell me about that first.'

'Guidi's family is well-off,' said Traúm, in the tone of someone remembering he has something to do.

'Did she tell you recently?'

Traúm nodded, noisily slurping up the last water from the mate tea, the part you don't normally drink.

'Can you believe it? They live in Israel. In Netanya. How come I never knew that?'

'I can't believe you didn't know that,' I said. 'You seem to know everything.'

Traúm was still thinking.

'Pass me the tea,' I asked him.

'They're embarrassed,' he said. 'That's why they haven't tried to get in touch. They're ashamed to have lost a son. They're so full of shame they're afraid to meet me.'

'How did Cristina know?'

'She's the one who knows everything. Forgetting is a job in itself: you have to note everything down carefully.'

'Note down everything that you want to forget?' I asked.

'It's not a contradiction,' said Traúm. 'I can't explain it, but it's not a contradiction. It's like when relatives need to see the body before they can accept the death of their loved one and start to heal. In the same way, to forget some people, you have to know what happened to them, right up to the end. Well, at least I know that Guidi's all right,' he said unexpectedly.

'Guidi's all right?' I said, taken aback.

'No,' said Traúm, and he went pale. 'I meant to say Guidi's family is all right. Guidi is dead,' he said.

I looked at the floor. Traúm shut his eyes.

I switched off the light, picked up the bottle of whisky, went into my bedroom, and as I was about to shut the door I heard Traúm say:

'Anyway, I'm never going to get over it.'

'Who knows?' I said, and fell onto my bed still dressed.

I took a sip of whisky. I liked the prospect of leaving next evening for Mar del Plata. God hadn't kept Esther by my side, but at least he was allowing me to flee her memory. I should have got up to shut the door but my legs refused to do my bidding. I'd walked a long way, I'd jumped over a wall, and I didn't want to let go of my bottle.

'It was the day of Benjamín's first mission,' said Traúm. 'What the fuck did they call it? Action? Operation? He had to kill someone. It wasn't a bomb; he had to shoot him. Guidi had managed to rent another apartment. It was an unfurnished flea pit. At the time he was sort of going out with Cristina. Benjamín had come to say his farewells and Guidi invited me along too. In those days we said good-bye to each other every day, all the time. Even as we spoke they could be coming into the building and kill all three of us, all four of us, in the time it takes to come up in the lift. But Benjamín came to say good-bye. Cristina was worried for him, and was kissing and touching Guidi. I'd already had Cristina, so I could see them touching each other without it getting to me too much. Benjamín had never slept with her.

'"Bye then," said Benjamín.

'"Wait," said Guidi. "Don't go so soon."

'"We'll see each other again," said Benjamín.

'"Doesn't matter," said Guidi. "Stay a bit longer."

'Benjamín, though, was heading for the door.

'"Wait," I said to him, and I wanted to add: "you're too young."

'But for some reason I couldn't say it. I couldn't take care of him.

'Benjamín took hold of the doorknob.

'"Come here," said Cristina.

'I'm sure Guidi whispered to Cristina to ask him back. If Cristina had been one of the sirens, Ulysses would never have been able to leave.

'Why did he ask Cristina to call him back? Maybe just for a moment Guidi caught a glimpse of the ignoble stupidity of the corner they'd backed themselves into. Maybe he suspected it was easier to save another than to save himself. That Benja, although he was just a few months younger, really was very young.

'Benja went over blindly to Cristina. Submissive.

'"I want to say goodbye to you," she told him.

'She took his face in her hands and gave him a lustful kiss on the mouth. Then she stroked his head. Benjamín let himself be stroked. How could he resist? He might die in a couple of hours. What was the point in holding back? Guidi smiled. Cristina started kissing them one after the other. At some point they called me over. I was sitting against a wall, just a few steps away, watching them. They invited me to join in the scene. I got the best part.'

I didn't ask what the best part was. I had an intuition, which is one of the least terrible ways of approaching knowledge.

'After that, Benjamín went off on his mission,' Traúm went on. 'His action, or his operation, whatever it was called. All those shit names. It might seem impossible but there are some words that are like a fetish: people feel important when they say them. I never feel important,' said Traúm. 'Not even when I sing the Hatikva, Israel's national hymn. I always feel like an idiot. That time, in my idiocy, I thought all that discreet and loving orgy was an attempt to keep Benja with us, to stop him from going, that we could keep him there. Later I discovered that Benjamín was even more obliged to go. This was the farewell to the warrior. His intuition was that they had given him this like an advance medal as a prize for the life he would give up for the "cause". And he couldn't say no. He couldn't go back. They'd given him his prize in advance. Cristina is a woman who offers herself to you like a last request. But I'm sure Guidi didn't want him to leave. Shall we get some sleep?'

Chapter thirty-three

I was woken up by the telephone. As I got out of bed I knocked the bottle of whisky over with my foot, and spilt the little bit of liquid still left—just a few drops.

Traúm wasn't on his chair anymore. I saw him ensconced in the kitchen, washed, hair combed, preparing a mate tea conscientiously and lovingly.

'Darling!' someone shouted down the phone.

'Esther?' I thought.

It was Gladis.

'You don't know how wonderful this is,' she told me.

'I know, I know,' I said.

Beyond her voice, which was like a jackdaw or a crow, you could hear the noise of the sea. She was speaking to me from the Rambla. Maybe she'd bought a mobile phone just so she could talk to me standing next to one of the two cement sea lions.

'I know Mar del Plata like the back of my hand.'

'I mean you don't know how wonderful it is for me,' said Gladis. 'How happy I am. The only thing missing is you.'

'I could turn up any time in the Bristol Hotel,' I said.

'I'm going to wait for you at the entrance to my beach tent,' she said, 'with my face down in the sand. I don't care if I swallow some sand.'

I was getting very excited.

'You have a good time,' I told her. 'Go and eat in The Old Sailor, right there on the Rambla.'

'All right, darling. I have to go because my card is running out.'

Traúm had finally managed to pour some of the lukewarm water into the pot for the mate tea.

'Listen,' I said to him. 'I know it's not something to talk about first thing in the morning. But it didn't occur to me last night. Can I ask you something?'

He sipped the tea through the metal straw and I saw a look of pain and annoyance on his face: he'd scalded himself.

I asked:

'How does Cristina's future husband know that the three of you served her mass? How could he have found out? Why are we assuming that's the reason he's so pissed off?'

'That's what I've been wondering ever since I got here. Did she tell him? Is it *vox populi*? But there's no other reason why he should feel such enthusiasm for getting me out of the way, that's for sure.'

'What if it's Cristina?' I said. 'What if she's playing a double game? Maybe she's as scared of you as she is of the past. She doesn't even want to see you. On the one hand she lets you have addresses for Benjamín and Guidi so you keep going ahead, on the other hand she's pushing you to leave. It wouldn't be so strange.'

'Look,' said Traúm reflectively, totally beside the point, 'Guidi's family lives in Israel.'

'Are you listening to what I'm saying?' I asked.

'So why does she want to see me in Mar del Plata?' he asked, coming back to the present.

'To beg you to leave. To ask you in person.'

'I don't think so,' said Traúm. 'Mar del Plata is the place for reconciliation.'

'Who told you that?' I shouted angrily.

'A friend,' said Traúm with a smile.

'You slept with my mother.' I couldn't stop myself from saying it, and in an accusing tone at that.

'No,' he said, with amiable seriousness. But it was a conditional negative, with potential risks. 'Do you know what the difference is between a gentleman, a Jew and a good Jew?' he asked me.

'Let me do the mate tea,' I answered.

'The difference lies in their sexual adventures. A gentleman is someone with no memory. A Jew is someone who dignifies the adventure by representing it in ethical fashion in his memory. And a good Jew has no adventures.'

I threw the mess of herbs and water that Traúm had managed to produce into the bin, and began to make a proper infusion.

'It's a lovely day,' said Traúm.

A few rays of light struggled through the miserable window of my apartment, which looked out onto nearby houses.

'I'm wondering,' he went on, 'if we wouldn't do better to go straight to Mar del Plata now and spend a lovely day like this on the beach. Then when it's time we can go meet her at the airport.'

'You'll have to pay a penalty for changing your flight. I'll have to pay a penalty too if I want to use this train ticket, because I've already missed the train it was booked for.'

'I'm more than happy to pay,' said Traúm. 'I don't think I'm going to stay in Argentina for much longer. How could I leave without having a dip at the Bristol Hotel?'

'Were you going to the Bristol too?' I asked.

'Strange question,' said Traúm. 'Next year in Jerusalem, next holiday in Miramar, next weekend at the Hotel Bristol. I'll pay for everything. You just call the travel agent.'

We had just one bag in which we put two pairs of bathing trunks. I took a baseball cap for me and some sunscreen which I wasn't planning to share.

'We'll buy our rubber rings there,' I said.

By two in the afternoon we were in Mar del Plata. Without

looking for a hotel we headed towards the Bristol. Traúm rented a beach tent and we left the bag there. We took turns to change behind the canvas curtain and went out onto the beach in our trunks.

Chapter thirty-four

I suppose there must be loads of cities where nothing changes. Since the 1950s Mar del Plata has been one of them. During the first decades of the twentieth century it was the refuge of the Creole oligarchy. It wavered towards the middle class at the end of the thirties, and was the beach of choice for the workers' unions during the Peronism of the forties through to the middle of the fifties. Ever since then it has kept up a gentle romance with the middle class. There is no lack of traitors who choose Punta del Este when they can, those who favour the tranquillity of Miramar, and those who turn up in Mar del Plata reluctantly, because they can't afford anything else. But the best of the middle class, and the Sephardic Jews of Once, know no better summer paradise than this magical and vulgar city. Many of them, with gold at their wrists and on the chains around their necks, sit under the umbrellas at the bottom of the gardens of the Bristol and spend all day playing cards, paying not the slightest attention to the sea. Golden stars of David glitter amongst the abundant white chest hair, together with small silver hands to ward off bad luck. mate tea circulates like a hookah pipe, and in their damp shade the umbrellas and beach tents, their feet buried in the sand, are reminiscent of a Middle Eastern souk. Traúm and I, however, chose a place where we could see the sea. We only had to step outside to feel ourselves roasted by the sun.

Traúm walked along the sandy path unhesitatingly towards an obese man sitting with his hands crossed over his paunch, bald, dark-skinned, with two symbols—a star of David and a hand to ward off bad luck—hanging on his chest. He was trying to read, I would guarantee with no success, a progressive current affairs magazine lying on the ground more than a metre from his face, the shiny pages reflecting the light of the sun with considerable violence. It was impossible for him to read it, but he was not going to get up and pick it up for anything in the world. He wasn't turning the pages either: he was staring at a page, which given the physical effort involved in reading it must have seemed interminable. If by a miracle he ever managed to finish it, he would doubtless wait for a breeze to waft in from the sea and turn the page for him.

When Traúm was near the man, he started to speed up until he achieved almost a trot. Once again I noticed how athletic he was. He was barely kicking up any sand and his feet seemed to slide along, rhythmic and harmonious.

'Dayan!' he shouted to the man, who looked up in surprise.

Without giving him time to react Traúm threw himself at the man, knocking over his chair, and both of them ended up in a heap on the sand. I feared for both of them.

This Dayan got up as best he could and looked at the face of his attacker. It's one thing to read an article invisible in the sunlight from your chair, and quite another to recognise someone you haven't seen for over twenty years. In the first trial the only thing that matters is the sight of the challenger, while in the second memory plays a decisive role. I sensed that Dayan found neither of these two things difficult.

He took Traúm's face in his hands, looked at him in amazement and cried:

'Elías. Where have you been?'

'In the wolf's mouth,' said Traúm.

'If you're not dead you must be fine,' said Dayan.

'I live in Israel,' said Elías.

'Mazel tov!' shouted Dayan.

'Let me introduce you to Elías,' said Traúm, pointing me out to his namesake. 'This man is the prophet of truth.'

'I sell cloth,' said Dayan, as if confirming his divine status.

Elías Dayan sold cloth in Calle Castelli. His face, his way of speaking, his job and the way he sat in his chair, even more than reality were all a perfect hologram to show to future generations how Sephardi Jewish businessmen had lived through the diaspora in Argentina. He was more than a person, he was an exemplar, a perfect model.

He'd known Guidi and Benjamín. He'd contributed money to the magazine through his business advertising.

'You have a star of David in the middle of your chest,' I said to him, not at all hostile, in friendly fashion. 'How come you gave money to a magazine called *God is silent?*'

'Because it's true,' said Dayan, grabbing hold of the star. 'God says nothing. If it hadn't been for David's shield, he would have killed us all. *Chazak veematz,*' he said, closing his fists.

'Be strong and brave,' Traúm translated for me.

'Why wouldn't I give them money?' went on Dayan, raising his hands to the sky, as if presenting them to God.

The sky was blue and clear, a light aircraft passed by trailing a banner advertising some sort of hand cream, and recalling a ghost of my childhood, when planes wrote smoke messages in the sky.

'Why wouldn't I give them money?' Dayan said again. 'I gave money for raffles, I gave money to my sons so they could throw it away, I threw money after women. Why wouldn't I give money to lads who studied the Torah?'

'But they were atheists,' I said. 'And anti-Zionists.'

When he heard the word 'anti-Zionist' Dayan's face twisted as if there was no worse insult, as if this was an insult not to be borne, a curse which should never be spoken.

He gestured with his hand, a manual 'pa!', dismissing my words.

'Nothing of the kind,' he said. 'They were good lads. They didn't know what they wanted. But they studied. They were all...what was it Guidi's grandmother used to say?'

Traúm was about to tell him, but Dayan remembered himself.

'*Yehudim tovim. Hakol yehudim tovim.*'

This left all three of us staring at the sea. You couldn't see it from Dayan's umbrella, but you could from the spot he had chosen to martyr his bald head and ruin his sight trying to read the magazine.

Traúm and Dayan could see Guidi and Banjamín running along the shore, their perfect boys' bodies and their bronzed skin. I could see them in their eyes. A boat passed, like another ghost from the past. Everything in Mar del Plata brings with it childhood and melancholy. Who knows, maybe in that boat were hidden Guidi and Benjamín, still boys, still with a chance to live, still with a chance to grow old. Maybe we had a chance to get them back if the boat compass would just point in the right direction. But if that happened, would they let themselves be saved? We could go further back in time than to a man who believes he is forging his own destiny.

'Once, Guidi got lost,' said Dayan, pointing to the shore. 'He went out with his sister to collect plastic cups. Guidi was seven years old and his sister nine. They went out along the shore to collect cardboard cups with Coca-Cola written on them. Only Coca-Cola, only cardboard and only along the shore. Guidi was already extraordinary. Anybody might have thought the sister was going with her little brother to help him with his collection, but in fact it was the other way round. It was Guidi who had come up with the three parameters: cardboard, the brand and the shore. He liked to classify things.'

Traúm nodded.

'Later on the sister came back alone. With "thousands" of cups, one inside the other. She had a whole line of them that seemed to reach up to the sky. It looked like the tower of Babel.

'"Where's Guidi?" their mother asked.

'"I don't know," said Berta, the sister.

'"What do you mean you don't know!" shouted their father. "You take your brother and then you don't bring him back?"

"'He ran off," said Berta. "He said he wanted to collect the cups and then he got bored. He started collecting stones. I carried on collecting cups. Suddenly I couldn't see him anymore."

'I was just a few steps away and I went over to them when I heard all the commotion,' Dayan went on. 'They were closer to the sea, number fifty-one. That one,' he pointed.

"The mother and father went out to look for him. The grandmother, grandfather, Berta and I stayed where we were, hoping he would come back riding piggyback on someone's shoulders amidst a round of applause. The grandmother was really anxious, and Berta couldn't stop crying. I was starting to get scared. The only person who seemed to be taking it calmly was the grandfather. But he wasn't calm, it was something else. He was a survivor of the Shoah, he had his number tattooed on his arm. At the time it was quite common to see Jews with their arm tattooed, along the beach here around the Bristol hotel. What was the grandfather, don Julio, thinking about? His name was Leivale, but he'd changed it to Julio in Argentina. He'd lost his first wife and his daughter in Poland. Fate decreed that he should lose sight of them when they were all sent to the concentration camp. What was going on in his head? Why wasn't he getting upset like the grandmother, why wasn't he desperate like the parents, why wasn't he crying like Berta, why wasn't he scared like me? I think he took it with the terrible calm of the man who is sure that God is silent. That He will go on beating him with no justification and no reward. That it makes no sense to suffer before going on suffering, or to go on suffering after you have suffered. That the same probability goes for the best and the worst, that death always has the last word and nobody can say anything back in reply. I'm not sure myself what I mean, but the grandfather didn't weep, and he wasn't upset.

'Things were looking bad. Guidi had gone missing at half two in the afternoon. It was five o'clock and there was no sign of him.

'Boris, Guidi's father, went to alert the police. And Luisa, the mother, went on walking right up to Punta Mogotes, at the far end of the beach.

'Police helicopers set out to look for Guidi...'

Dayan and Traúm looked at each other in a sinister pause.

'They searched for him along the whole beach,' Dayan went on.

'The sun started to go down at seven in the evening. I remember I was particularly struck by the fact that people started to leave the beach. It was as if the match was already over and there was nothing else to be done.

'The grandmother was sobbing uncontrollably. Berta had fallen asleep out of exhaustion. The grandfather was making patterns in the sand with his foot, and I think he was praying. But without making a show of it. I stayed with them.

'By eight o'clock there was hardly anybody left on the beach. The police helicopters had searched from one end to the other without finding anything. All the lifeguards had been alerted. No sign of Guidi.

'Luisa came back, desperate. She was crying, too. She just managed to blurt out:

'"At least I want to see his body. I want the sea to give me back his body."

'I feared something worse than the sea, that some pervert had kidnapped him.

'Who could say?' Dayan stopped.

His eyes were full of tears.

'The police persuaded the parents to go back to the hotel. There was no point staying there on the beach. The hotel was a better place to celebrate any good news they might be able to bring. Luisa didn't want to go, but Boris convinced her.

'"I swear, señora," the policeman told her, "we won't stop until we find him."

'He didn't say but I could read between the lines—dead or alive.

'"Does the boy know the name of the hotel?"

'"Yes," said Luisa. "The name and where it is."

'"Go on back to the hotel then," said the policeman. "It's the best place to wait for any news."

'Boris took her by the arm and almost dragged her along. We

all got into Boris' car. We looked like a funeral cortege. There was space for me because Guidi was missing. My wife and my kids went back to the hotel on their own, on foot, terribly upset.

'Luisa couldn't bring herself to go into the hotel. It seemed to her as though going in was giving up, accepting that her son was dead, the most dreadful of losses.

'Boris persuaded her again. He spoke firmly but kindly to her.

'Luisa went into the hotel and I heard her cry out. It was a cry to split the heavens. I never heard a cry like that again in all my life. It was a biblical cry. When we Jews lived our epic, the women must have cried out like that.

'We all ran in behind her.

'In the hotel foyer, happy and without a care in the world, with a table laid just for him, looked after and clucked over by the hotel managers, Guidi was eating slices of toast with condensed milk.

'Luisa was shouting with joy, she was crying, she was thanking God.

'It was a wonderful thing to see this mother hugging her child.

'By now we were all crying. The most extraordinary thing was the grandfather. He threw himself to the floor, was kissing the floor, then he would raise his head and kiss the floor again.

'He couldn't bring himself to hug Guidi, he would go up to him and then stop a few steps away, as if the boy were a gleaming light that couldn't be approached. As if by hugging him you would make him vanish in a puff of smoke between your fingers. As if for his son Boris to be able to hug his grandchild, he would have to deprive himself of the pleasure of hugging him. There was no unfinished business with God anymore. He didn't owe God anything, and God didn't owe him anything either. He didn't even ask him to let him hold his own grandchild.

'Guidi had gone on walking towards Punta Mogotes. A lifeguard found him. Bright as he was, Guidi had no sense of direction and he never got tired. He had no idea how far he had walked. In Punta Mogotes the lifeguard from one of the bathing establishments found him, hoisted him up on his shoulders and took him along a couple of stretches of beach to see if his family was there. But he'd gone much further than that, much much further. Guidi had no idea how far he had gone. The lifeguard, a woman, kept him in her hut until she could find out where he was from. By one of those strange chances, there was a photographer on this part of the beach who was staying in the same hotel as Guidi, and he recognised him. The lifeguard said the best thing was to take him straight back to the hotel, because the boy couldn't say where his parents were. He knew the name of the hotel and where that was, but he didn't know which beach they were on. Her shift was coming to an end and when she saw her replacement turn up and sit in the lifeguard's seat, the high-up one, she went by car with the photographer and Guidi, without telling her colleague. When the police came and questioned the new lifeguard, he didn't know anything. Guidi was already safe and sound back in the hotel. And so on.'

'Guidi was saved that time,' said Dayan.

'In any case, God is silent,' said Traúm.

'But there's another bit to that story,' said Dayan, annoyed at Traúm's interruption.

Dayan was the kind of storyteller who demands your complete attention and is irritated by anybody who shows the slightest sign of joining in. He always had his hand held in the air as if to say, 'I haven't finished yet.'

'There's a postscript to the story. It's like a piece of fiction.

'The next day we all went back to the Bristol hotel. It was as if nothing had happened. The waves still came in on the beach, the sky was still crystal clear, the grandfather was playing dominoes with a man who did not have a tattoo on his arm. Only Berta looked as though she was convalescent, slightly anxious. And then as Guidi was talking to his father, he raised his voice and we heard him say:

'"Pah, everyone says I got lost. Everyone says I got lost. But I'd never been to Punta Mogotes. I didn't get lost—I discovered a new place."

'The grandfather answered, looking up from a domino piece that wasn't going to win him the game:

"'You didn't discover a new place," he told him, and added sententiously: "You got lost."

'Guidi replied with all the clumsy pride of a child prodigy of seven. He asked in a boastful tone of voice:

"'And so what's the difference between getting lost and discovering a new place?"

"'Knowing how to get back," his grandfather replied.

Chapter thirty-five

Dayan's wife appeared and stood stock-still, like a statue of salt. She was looking at the past. She managed to recover herself and gave Traúm a kiss on both cheeks. She was a woman of around sixty, some five years or so younger than her husband. But amongst her wrinkled tanned hips and the ebony colour of her breasts she still bore traces of the woman she had been. I always imagine in women of Sephardic origin a war and sumptuous dance which could tear me away from the useless melancholy of the Russian and Polish steppes of three quarters of my ancestors.

That reminded me of something and I asked them to excuse me. I managed to avoid the tea and *churros* that were starting to rain down on Traúm and that the Dayans ate from lunchtime onwards without a pause. It was a constant feast on the beach.

I walked a little way along the sand and looked between the umbrellas and tents grouped just under the cement sea lion. I saw families with the old folks chatting, woman left on their own, then finally I spotted her. Gladis was sunbathing on her front, with her eyes shut. Her gigantic white arse rose up like a marine animal which has been given permission to come and spend a few hours on the beach. I dropped down on top of her without a word, in a horribly uncomfortable position. I took great pleasure in the astonished faces of the married couple opposite, who saw an intruder jump on top of a woman alone.

Gladis had a moment of bewilderment and fear, but I whispered something dreadful into her ear and she answered me gleefully:

'You came!' she yelled, 'You came!'

'Shhh,' I murmured.

Then I said something else to her and we moved back into the shade of her tent.

'That's great that you hired a tent,' I said.

'Just in case you came,' she said.

We squashed in as best we could behind the canvas curtain that protects the intimacy of these tent tenants. Being so short she managed to lie down, though a foot stuck out the other side. I moulded myself to her mound of flesh, to that malleable prime matter.

'Are you never going to do it to me any other way?' she asked me in a whisper into my ear.

'That would create an intimacy that wouldn't be appropriate,' I said, setting to work. 'Our relationship is based on this essential distance.'

There was a grain of truth in what I said. My movements were slow, majestic. She took it all. I was happy. Only contempt for another reserves similar pleasure for us. Because I wanted to live with Esther and die by her side. But only with Gladis the whale—precisely because I would never do anything more than this with her—could I attain the heights of primitive man, sexual dominion, absolute possession and total disinterest for the creature at my feet who was totally mine. I worked her with pleasure and delight. I reconstructed that part of her body as you model a sculpture out of precious material, malleable like the damp sand of the shore, soft as a new skin and valuable as marble.

But there was no getting away from the bother of the dry sand.

Gladis never reached climax, but she enjoyed the whole thing. She was having a good time.

'I love you,' I said into her ear.

She didn't answer. In that chance moment her face was screwed up in a swift grimace of pain.

Chapter thirty-six

Gladis said she had to go to the hotel to wash and get changed. I suggested doing it in the sea. She told me she needed a good wash and clean clothes. She asked me to look after her things.

'I have to go and work,' I told her.

'Are you never going to stay a little bit?' she asked me.

'I don't want to condemn you to a relationship that can have no future,' I said.

'Give me a kiss,' she asked, offering me her fat, colourless lips.

'You know I can't,' I told her.

'One day...' said Gladis, and she didn't finish the sentence. She set off up the Rambla with her usual gait of a person with problems.

'One day,' I continued her sentence, 'the Messiah will come. But not even then will unrequited lovers find peace.'

I waited for her to disappear up the street, obscured from view by the sea lions, I told myself that she had nothing of any real value for anybody to steal, and headed to the water to clean myself up. I threw myself into the water like a dead weight and washed myself clean of Gladis and the tales of death that Traúm was telling me as if he was the verbally incontinent keeper of a cemetery. The earth of his dead friends' graves had mixed in with the air in my lungs.

Talking to him was like a lengthy *kaddish*—but wasn't that the same with all Jews of his age? Luckily a large part of the Sephardi Jews still had a twentieth-century Jewish history devoid of repeated pogroms, with no Shoah, and with no wild-eyed sons who killed or were gunned down in a lost continent, where no Yiddish or Hebrew was spoken. The bulk of Sephardi Jews still kept, like some sort of treasure, a forgotten secret: how to be a Jew without a Shoah.

But the sea knew nothing of these things. Like unrequited love, it was always the same, and nothing would change it. The salt filled me with euphoria and I remembered my grandmother who would stand by the water's edge scooping up foam and rubbing it over her body, praising the virtues of iodine.

'Iodine,' I said to myself, heading back to the shore and gathering up some foam in my hand.

'Iodine,' I said again as the foam evaporated. My grandmother knew.

I walked and walked along the water's edge. I might have been Guidi. When she came back Gladis wouldn't find me there. I knew how to get back, but today I didn't want to. How far did I walk? Like Guidi, as far as Punta Mogotes. The sight of the Argentine women in swimming costumes raised my spirits. I wanted more and more. A German shepherd dog ran out of nowhere and started chasing me. I ran into the sea in a panic and heard a blonde woman calling him. The top-level Nazi chiefs had been reincarnated as German shepherds. They roamed over the earth in search of the remaining Jews. Once again, as at the beginning of the Exodus, God closed the doors of the sea against the enemy and opened them to his people. I came out of the water a few metres further on to see the blonde woman throwing the dog a 'bagel' (maybe it was a frisbee, but my father had got me into the habit of calling anything circular that flew over the sand on the beach a bagel; if at any point we'd seen a UFO my father, beyond a shadow of a doubt, would have exclaimed, 'Look, there's a bagel'). The dog would take it back to her joyfully and both of them were smiling, the blonde and the dog. Coca-Cola sellers were passing by—the bedouins of Mar del Plata. With their backpack cool boxes and red clothes. Who bothers to note down in the book of human achievement the endless walking of soft drink sellers along the Argentine coast, ploughing their way up and down the burning sands, kilometre after kilometre, under a merciless sun, their lips cracked by the salty air? I found some children playing, like me, by the edge of the water, the older brothers hitting the younger ones, the little girls drawing hearts in the sand that the sea would wipe out, and a fat woman who jumped up, ran a kilometre over to her little girl and gave her a loud whack to stop her putting a grain of sand in her mouth. The human race in all its splendour. But nothing too serious.

When I reached the edge of Punta Mogotes I sat down as if I had arrived somewhere. I didn't know how long I'd been away, but the sun was beginning to go down. I thanked God for that day, for letting me see Gladis, for saving me from the dog and for making me fit and strong enough to walk from one end of Mar del Plata to the other. Where was Traúm, where had we rented our own bit of space?

But I wasn't Guidi: I knew how to get back. Maybe the sky would fall on my head, but I wasn't prepared to declaim cheerfully that I would willingly give my life up for the life of a stranger. Or to take his either.

I walked steadily on. I retraced my steps as the day drew to a close. The fish were coming close into the shore again. The Coca-Cola sellers were taking off their nomads' portable coolers, removing their sandals and letting their feet sink into the nighttime sea. The sandwich seller was playing roulette by himself, to decide his own fate. The last light aircraft was going home, trailing a banner advertising a circus that no one was looking at. And Javier Mossen was returning to the tales of the dead.

I reached the Bristol Hotel—Traúm's beach tent, not Gladis'— when the air was filled with that lovely grey that you're not sure comes from the moon or the sun, which might have the same origin but are not the same.

While it is a light that doesn't invite you to live, it doesn't make life difficult either. A light which could keep you on the beach indefinitely.

Both Dayan and Traúm had gone but in our tent, number 51, I found the bag we had brought with us. I looked around for Traúm—fearing that perhaps he had got lost on the beach as well—and I saw a man crouching down on the strip of damp sand that separates the dry sand from the sea.

Beside him two short tongues of flame seemed to rise up out of the sand.

'That's it,' I said, 'he's gone mad.'

I quickly went over to him.

'A volcano,' said Traúm. 'You dig a bit of a hole, and put newspaper in it. Over the hole, all around it, a little mound of sand. One side of the hole you dig out a bit more, like a tunnel. You pass a twist of paper through the tunnel as a wick. You can put alcohol on it if need be. I know how to light it without alcohol. We used to do it.'

A plastic lighter was lying on the ground in between the two small volcanoes. I didn't ask him if he had borrowed it from Dayan or if he had bought it.

'Two volcanoes,' I said to him.

Traúm gazed at them as if he was still praying. Two fires burning swiftly in the night, with no witnesses.

'That's enough,' I said angrily. 'They're dead. Every day boys the same age as them die. Let's say they went to Israel, like you wanted them to. They might have died in the Six-Day War, or the war of Yom Kippur, or the war in Lebanon, maybe a terrorist would have caught them with a bomb on a bus. Get it into your head that they died in peace like good Jews, and leave it at that.'

'But they didn't die in peace,' said Traúm. 'They didn't die in peace. I know anyone can die, at any time. Right now a huge wave could come up onto the beach and wash us away. But how you die changes things. It changes things. They didn't die in peace, not only because they were killed but because they didn't know how to die. They ruined their own lives with the way they died. Murdered people are an object, out there. But I'm not talking about them. I couldn't take care of them.'

I was silent. I was tired of so much death, but I couldn't find a delicate way of telling him. I had no tact.

Traúm came back to himself. At our feet the volcanoes were small and looked pretty insignificant. But when we got back to our tent the sea still hadn't put them out.

'Let's wait another hour and then we'll head out to the airport,' Traúm told me.

The attendant came over and told us we had to leave the tent. We took turns to get changed behind the canvas sheet, putting on long trousers and sandals. Traúm gave me back the bathing costume I had lent him. I picked up the bag and we headed to the Rambla.

We stopped at one of the little bars and ordered Fernet with Coca-Cola for both of us.

I had sand all over me that was irritating me, but Traúm looked as though he had just showered. As if he was used to going into the desert and had discovered a way of staying sand free when he got back to civilisation.

'Benjamín...' he began.

Seeing my face, he stopped. My expression was a silent repeat of my previous request—enough.

'This is the last story,' he told me.

I nodded, I don't know whether out of understanding or curiosity. I was surprised that this Jew in the desert, who could climb walls with the agility of a monkey, had the memory of an elephant and the precision of a mathematician, was lowering himself to ask me the one thing he's really been asking ever since we met—to let him tell his final story.

'Benjamín had just lost his father,' he told me.

'When are we talking about?' I asked him.

I had lost my father eighteen years before, and I was sure that right up to my dying day I would feel as though I had only just lost him.

'When he started becoming inflexible,' Traúm told me. 'He lost his father at the moment of greatest Marxist politicisation, or whatever you want to call it. I'm telling you this because we came to Mar del Plata once. One weekend. That's why it's come back to me.

This is the last thing I'll tell you. We were walking along the shore, just him and me. Guidi was in the hotel. I asked Benjamín what he remembered about his father.

'"We're all going to die one day," Benjamín said to me. "Death is just a stage in matter. We are all matter."

'"We also have a soul," I said. "Anyway, all I'm asking is for you to tell me something about him."

'"You're only asking me because he's just died," Benjamín told me. "But do you know how many people died the same day, of hunger, of an oppressor's bullet, in the prisons of dictators?"

'"But it's your dad that's just died," I told him. "Any human being who loses his father feels sorrow and has something to tell. What's the matter with you, Benjamín?"

'"What's the matter with you?" he asked me. "Can't you see what's happening all around you? You're still talking to me as if I was a kid, one of the three musketeers. I don't need your comfort."

'I shut up, thinking I had lost my friends forever. Thinking that Benjamín really had turned into matter.

'Then, after a long pause, he said:

'"My dad was very fat. When I was a boy he often got home after I had already gone to bed. But I couldn't go to sleep until I heard him come in, until I heard the door close in the way only he closed it. He didn't bang it but shut it firmly in a way I could always recognise. And I thought that as he was fat he was going to protect us. Then I could go to sleep, because my fat daddy was at home looking after us."

'That was the last thing he ever said to me,' concluded Traúm. 'I mean, we spoke a lot more. He came out with a lot of rubbish. But that was the last thing he really said to me.'

Traúm looked at his watch. It was time to head out to the airport.

Chapter thirty-seven

The ground along the covered part of the Rambla has its own particular damp smell. It's a mixture of the water they use to wash it down, disinfectant, and air trapped beneath the thick cement domes. You can walk down the Rambla and breathe it in, but it is not the smell of the sea or the roughness of the sand that is offered here. In the middle of nature this brute cement structure imposes itself forcefully. It's curious to say the least that right next to the sea you can savour the unpleasant damp odour given off by concrete. Traúm was already walking along the esplanade, in the open air. I went a little further along under this weighty roof.

We took a taxi to the airport. It was already dark.

We reached Camet airport at half past eight. At nine o'clock Cristina's flight was due to arrive. Or leave, I don't know. They were supposed to meet on the runway.

'Wait for me here,' said Traúm.

And he vanished. In a flash he'd disappeared. How he managed to melt into thin air, I still don't know to this day, but it was skills like that that had saved his life on a number of occasions over the years. He was no architect. Later he took the trouble to give me a hint as to the profession in which all his prodigious abilities found their outlet.

I sat down on one of the plastic seats. Two security men were guarding the access to the runway and there was no way I was going to put them to the test. I didn't have the slightest intention of following Traúm wherever he had gone, no way. Where was he? On the runway? I still had the sand-smeared bag in my hand. I opened it and looked for a magazine, one that Traúm had bought during my walk along the shore. But all I could find were sandals and bits of beach. I walked over to a kiosk and bought a comic strip magazine.

Why hadn't Traúm let me in on his plan, how much longer would he be? Why that 'wait for me here' with no other explanation? All of a sudden I didn't care anymore. Traúm's destiny was out of my hands now, that was for sure, way out of my reach. Traúm had started to do exactly as he wanted: you can't take care of a healthy adult. Only when you're not trying.

I read the comic strips and found myself more interested in the activities of the characters in the stories that in those of Traúm himself. There's no better way to wait for someone than to forget all about him. One day scientists will find the strange fluid that the mind secretes into time and time into the mind: the person we are waiting for comes back faster the less we think about him.

I'd read the last strip and barely twenty minutes had gone by. I put the magazine down on the seat next to me and started looking at the people around me. A man dressed in a suit passed by me followed by his wife wearing a short white skirt, and his son, still in his swimming trunks. He was almost certainly heading back to work after a few days' holiday, while his family were staying on in Mar del Plata for a few more weeks. The woman was thick-set but shapely, and her face displayed the features of the typical housewife. Her buttocks were firm, she moved them without swaying and they wouldn't have caught the attention of most men at that time and in that country, but I was attracted. As the woman moved—whether leaning down to speak to her son or helping her husband with his case—you could see right up to the end of her arse, or the beginning, pressed into a yellow bikini with black stripes which took the place of panties. I thought that for this man on his way back to work, this woman must be a weary habit, while if I came across her on a bed with white sheets with no blankets or covers, I would think of her as a miraculous gift. I really wanted her to be a housewife whose husband was bored with her, while nobody except me knew how to find a unique treasure there underneath her bikini.

'Excuse me, can I borrow this magazine?'

A little girl of about five had picked up the comic that I had left on the seat beside me.

'Of course,' I told her.

Her mother, a dried-up, ugly blonde dressed for the office, sat down and the child immersed herself in the magazine.

It was a comic strip about the television programme The Simpsons, and had two episodes. In one of them, Homer, the father of the Simpsons, was dying over the course of a couple of drawings. He went through Paradise and through Hell, then, thanks to electric shock to his heart, he came back to Earth.

'Mum, Homer's dying,' the child said to her mother.

The mother took the magazine, looked at me suspiciously as if I was guilty of something, and said:

'No, he's not dying. He's asleep.'

'He's dying,' repeated the child. 'Are we going to die in the plane too?'

The woman laughed out loud.

'No, darling,' she told her. 'We're not going to die in the plane. Give the man back his magazine, we have to go.'

'You can keep it,' I said.

'Give it back to him,' the woman insisted.

Reluctantly the girl gave me back the magazine and said:

'Here you are. Thank you very much.'

They disappeared.

I sat there for a few moments thinking about the little girl, her mother, the housewifely buttocks. All this was the flux of life. This chaotic, tender and mediocre journey that was the best way to live. Mothers took care of their children and feared death. Women kept their secret attraction and men had to dress to go to work. Not much more than this could be extracted from the surface of life: we had to look for the peaks in deserted corners without telling or bothering anybody. Poor Pesce, inside his wretched existence, had found an honourable way out, acknowledging that his madness was morally unacceptable rather than setting out to convince the world of his point of view.

I sat thinking about all this for a long time. I was feeling serious, I was not suffering. I liked the air-conditioning of the airport and the coming and going of the passengers didn't bore me. Each human stamp had something to tell me.

Suddenly, as if the hall was a low-budget studio, an unlikely soap opera scene, the door of the gents' toilet opened and Traúm came out.

Chapter thirty-eight

Traúm passed by me like a comet that I would have to follow. He didn't say a word. I got up without picking up the magazine and almost ran after him. He flagged down a taxi and gave me barely a few seconds to get in: nobody would have said he bothered to wait for me to climb in. He banged the door shut and ordered the driver to head back to the coast.

All of a sudden the sky clouded over, and inside the taxi the silence was heavy.

'Have you come from Buenos Aires?' asked the driver.

I mumbled a yes.

Traúm smelt of a woman's perfume. He smelt of Cristina.

There was the sound of a thunderclap and Traúm told the taxi driver to stop.

We were at one of the viewpoints of the whole city, just a few steps away from the place where Alfonsina Storni had let herself be swallowed up by the sea. If the rain promised by the dark sky were to come down now, Traúm and I would also die, drowned on our feet.

We sat on the concrete wall that looks over the sea, about ten metres above the sand.

'It's Friday today,' I said. 'The Sabbath.'

All the stars were ready and waiting, but the clouds had covered them over once again. I looked up and tried to find at least three.

Traúm chided me as if I was doing something foolish. I looked at him and in the dim light of nighttime I saw a smile on his face.

'It's dangerous to count the stars,' he said. 'That's one of the ways the Inquisition used to expose the *marranos*, the ones who went on practicing in secret. When the officials of the Holy Office saw a man looking up and pointing a finger towards the sky, they knew he was a Jew calculating whether the Sabbath had finished or not. Off to the pyre with him.'

I nodded and went on with my search. I found at least three stars and counted them defiantly.

Traúm laughed.

'Have you got a Sabbath story for me?' I asked.

'I don't know if it's good enough,' he said, 'but it's the only one I've got.'

And he told me about his meeting with Cristina amongst the cargo planes at Camet airport.

It was Casablanca, there were no two ways about it.

Cristina got off a plane which had just the pilot still on board. Traúm waited for her, his hands in his pockets, expecting a message, a revelation or a pretext. She threw herself at him and kissed him full on. She put his hands on her breasts, her hips against his, her tongue down his throat. She teased him, provoked him, squeezed him. I understood that Traúm had kissed her naked breast. He didn't spell it out but I gathered she put his hand under her skirt and under her panties too. These things were said in Hebrew. Who knows whether they were words of love or obscenities. Who knows, maybe they insulted each other? Insults in Hebrew are strange and serious. They are devastating, biblical insults. They are the insults of an angry God. I don't know how things went on after that, but along the side of the runway there is enough vegetation to conceal two naked bodies. In any case Traúm didn't seem agitated, he wasn't covered in dirt or sweat, and the only smell to come off him was the sweet elegance of women.'

'Who's after us then?' I asked.

'The husband,' said Traúm. 'And for the reason we guessed.'

'Who told him?' I asked anxiously.

Traúm laughed a loud laugh.

I gestured to him to go on.

A drop fell from the sky.

'Who told him?' I repeated.

'It's incredible,' said Traúm.

'If it starts pouring before you've told me, I'll never speak to you again in my life,' I said.

'It's already started,' said Traúm.

'It's just a few drops still.'

'I've already counted five,' said Traúm.

'It's dangerous to count drops of rain,' I said. 'You'd do better to tell me what happened.'

'She told him,' said Traúm. 'They tell each other stories to get themselves excited. He likes her to tell him stories. Bit by bit, without any idea what it would lead to, she told him the story of her and three of us, with Guidi and Benjamín. She told him as if it was just one of the many erotic stories that got the two of them going. But she repeated it, or told it in a particular way. He guessed it was true. And she couldn't claim it was made up. She tried to stop him but she couldn't. Can you imagine anything more ridiculous?'

'Yes,' I said, 'absolutely.'

'A story she would like to have kept tucked away forever and she hid it the best way of all, by telling it as if it was a story. But she couldn't keep it up. And señor Reches set the dogs loose, you can see why. But what do you make of her? Why did she do it?'

'Once,' I said, 'I was told to write an article on crimes of passion, with quotes from people involved. Since I don't like to write about the real tragedies of people who are still alive, I hunted through the archives and filled the piece with notorious cases over the last century. There are loads of them. But Pesce made me get examples from real recent cases. He wanted a man who had killed his wife the month before, or a woman who had put rat poison in her incestuous brother's tea when she found out she was pregnant. I did what I always do on these occasions: I made it up.

'I invented a young Argentine who lived in Brazil. He gets together with a young lady, falls in love and kills her when he realises she's a transvestite. A kind of Madame Butterfly mixed in with a real case I had come across, but which ended in suicide rather than murder.

'Pesce loved it, the whole thing, the name, the age of the man. But he wanted a photo. Pesce didn't know, or didn't want to know, that the evidence was invented, and he wanted a photo. Where was I going to find a face that would fit a story like that? I spent a night tossing and turning and then decided: my source would not agree to any photographs.

'He agreed to give his first name and his age, but he refused to give his surname or his face. That's all he would do.

'I'd made my decision but there was still a technical problem,' I continued. 'I'd found it very easy to invent the story on paper, but I found it much tougher to lie to Pesce's face when I told him my source didn't want any photos. I could give my made-up story to Pesce on paper, but lying in person was a skill I never acquired.'

'What did you do?' asked Traúm.

Neither of us said it, but the rain had run out of patience.

'I called a friend, I asked him to take up the story, but he should refuse to give me his surname or his photo.'

'Did you get him to call Pesce?'

'No. I just said to him: "I have something crazy to ask you. Listen to this story, pretend it happened to you. Ok. Now I'll ask you for a photograph to go with the piece. Would you give it to me? No. Thanks a lot." And that was that.'

'But why did you do that?'

'I needed to have a grain of truth in what I said, so I could lie better to Pesce. Obviously I couldn't ask any of my friends—and none of them would have accepted anyway—to pretend in public that this made-up tragedy had happened to them. But all I needed was to imagine it had happened to him and get him to refuse to give his surname and a photo, and that way I could say something of the truth. That's what literature is: it needs a grain of truth in the story.'

'What about stories from the bedroom?' asked Traúm, as if he knew nothing about this kind of thing.

'Most, unfortunately,' I said, 'don't work without a large grain of truth in them. The problem is that the grain of truth can become the whole truth. And the whole truth, in bed, doesn't work. Nor in literature either.'

We had to get a taxi.

Chapter thirty-nine

We ended up in a bar near the Provincial Hotel. I didn't know this would be our last meeting.

The bar was lit with a yellow light and I was pale, like a man suffering from an unknown illness. It was a nasty yet somehow gentle light.

We were side by side, next to each other at the bar. It was not far off eleven o'clock.

Traúm reached into his pocket and pulled out a damp plastic envelope. He put it on the table. A ticket holder.

He pressed the little plastic popper and took out a ticket. He let me see it. Buenos Aires to Tel Aviv.

I looked at the date.

'It leaves at eight o'clock tomorrow morning!' I exclaimed.

'Cristina gave it to me,' said Traúm.

'What are you going to do?'

'The last flight to Buenos Aires leaves at twelve o'clock tonight. I'll be on it. I'll go to the Juncal Hotel to pick up my luggage, then taxi back to the airport. I'll have a few glasses in the bar. I'll buy a book, have a seat and at eight o'clock I'll be on my way back to Israel.'

'So never mind all my requests for you to leave. This harlot gives you a ticket and off you go.'

'Does that seem so bad to you?'

'It seems perfect. But you should understand why I feel so vulnerable.'

The two of us smiled. I looked out of the window as if to rest my eyes for a moment. When I came back, I had a question.

'Why did you tell me all this, Traúm?'

We hadn't ordered yet. The waiter was keeping his eye on us as if we were two beggars who might run off with the table. We were soaked from head to foot and gazing at each other like two lovers.

'What shall we have?' asked Traúm. 'Apparently beer makes you cold. Whisky makes you drunk. A tea?'

'Two teas,' I said to the waiter.

Traúm was resting his chin on his two clasped hands.

'Who else would I tell?' said Traúm. 'When you called I felt you were genuinely worried for me. You really did feel responsible. If anything had happened to me, you would have suffered. You felt responsible for me. Who else would I tell my story?'

'Am I a good Jew?' I asked.

'A washed-up Jew,' said Traúm.

The tea arrived.

'I'm not an architect,' said Traúm after the first sip.

I burnt myself.

'I was working for Israel,' he said.

'In what way?' I asked.

'Looking after adults,' he said. 'I tried to look after Guidi and Benjamín. But I couldn't, because they knew I wanted to look after them. So I stayed near them to get information, to look after other adults: the ones lucky enough not to know they were being looked after.'

'I don't understand,' I said.

'Through Guidi and Benja, I was gathering information on the Montoneros,' he said.

'You were working for...?' I said, struck dumb.

Traúm nodded before I said the word, stopping me from saying it.

'Did Guidi and Benja know?' I asked.

Traúm shook his head.

'I tried to look after them,' he said.

'And what did you do with the information you got?' I asked, shaking a little.

'I never had to use it. But those were the years of the kindergarten in Maalot, and we already knew they were arm in arm with Arafat. We needed information. All that dies with me: I didn't use it. Anyway, it was stuff I would only have used outside this country: it would never have got into the hands of the people who killed Guidi and Benja.'

The teas had stopped steaming. The silence was a different colour from the light which sullied the bar. The waiter seemed to be walking on tiptoe.

'My dear friend,' said Traúm, and he held out his hand to me.

I didn't take it.

At that moment I felt I could have kissed him on the mouth. Not because it was a homosexual love—although we were gazing at each other like two lovers—but because it was a kind of love that friendship, a shaking of hands, could not express.

I got up and stepped towards him. There was nothing more than a small café table between us, but it seemed like a long walk to me.

We held each other very tight.

I don't know why but I began to weep against his shoulder.

'My dad would be surprised at me,' I said into his ear.

'I'm very glad I met you,' Traúm said to me.

I finally stopped crying and let him go.

'This is the moment when I should give you your orders as the fourth musketeer, like D'Artagnan,' said Traúm, as I tried to mop up my running nose with those little napkins that absorb next to nothing.

He got up and left. Without paying.

I didn't watch as he disappeared into the street, nor did I look for his silhouette as it hailed a taxi.

I called the waiter over to pay and caught his look, which said: queer.

Chapter forty

I'm sure I will never see Traúm again. And that he won't exist in that form for much longer. At some point his surname will change, his Argentine identity will disappear, maybe he'll even forget Spanish forever. His name will mean nothing to those who never met him in person, and those who did meet him will have every reason to want to forget him. Maybe his last move before saying good-bye to his birth name would be to visit Guidi's family in Netanya. I don't know.

Maybe he will repeat his name once more before dying, maybe he'll repeat the names of all three of them, the three musketeers.

Dramatic as it sounds, this is a small story. The story of a man who came back to say *kaddish* for his two dead friends? The story of a journalist who sealed the trunk of his endless doubts with a tragic tale? It was certainly a small story that couldn't be pigeonholed.

As for me, I left the bar with the bag and ran to call Esther, from the telephones along the covered stretch of the Rambla. The cement pathway, empty and drenched with water, was gloomy.

Why was I calling her? What if a man answered? Why was I trying my luck? Why didn't I call her from a nicer place? She answered herself, and when I said 'hallo' the sound echoed around me shamelessly.

'I love you, Esther,' I told her.

She didn't answer.

'Esther, I want to have children with you. You're the only woman in the world I want to have children with. Who are you going to have children with?'

There was a long pause, then she said in a slightly sardonic voice:

'That's right. I hadn't thought about that.'

'Do what you like with me,' I said. 'Whatever you want. I'm never going to touch another woman in my life.'

Esther laughed.

'I don't know if I want you to promise me that,' she said.

Once more I was weeping like an idiot.

'To start with you can bring me back a stick of rock.'

'Fine,' I said. 'What else?'

'For the first year I want complete control of the remote and I get to choose all the videos.'

I swallowed hard.

'Fine,' I said. 'Now come here.'

'Where's here??' she asked.

'Mar del Plata,' I said.

Esther thought for a moment.

'Are we going to spend the weekend in Mar del Plata?'

'Get a plane, I'll pay for it. I'll call you in an hour to tell you which hotel I'm staying in.'

'This is all too fast,' said Esther.

'Mar del Plata is the ideal place for reconciliation,' I said.

Another silence from Esther.

'We'll have to move,' she said.

'Wherever you like,' I said. 'An apartment, a house in the country. Wherever you like.'

'Call me in an hour. I'm going to see if I can find anybody still awake who can tell me about flights to Mar del Plata.'

'I love you,' I told her.

We hung up.

I walked down the covered Rambla and realised how stupid I had been. What if Esther came and we chanced to bump into Gladis, and the fatty threw herself at me and spoilt everything?

I walked out from under the cover and headed towards the pedestrian walkway, without trying to shield myself from the rain.

About the Author

Marcelo Birmajer

Marcelo Birmajer is one of South America's most prominent young writers. He has written over 20 books and screenplays for some of Argentinean cinema's most important films. His unique style, a combination of Latin machismo, self-irony and Jewish humor, has earned him the title "The Woody Allen of Pampas."

His collected *Stories of Married Men* will be published by *The* Toby Press next year.

The fonts used in this book are from the Garamond family

The Toby Press publishes fine writing,
available at leading bookstores everywhere. For more
information, please visit www.tobypress.com